This Book was placed in the Church Library

IN MEMORY OF

Margaret (Peg) McCuen

by Devon & Virginia Hoseler

WHISPER THE ROBIN

WHISPER THE ROBIN

BERNARD PALMER

ZONDERVAN PUBLISHING HOUSE
A Division of the Zondervan Corporation
Grand Rapids, Michigan

*To our close personal friend
and brother in Christ,
BARNEY LACENDRE,
who opened up the ways
of his people to us in a way
we would not have believed possible.
His experiences, especially as a
spirit worshiper in the days before
his conversion, formed the basis
for much of this novel.*

Preface

For ten summers my wife and I have lived close to the Cree in northern Saskatchewan, Canada. We have visited their isolated villages and have spent countless hours talking with veteran missionaries and both Christian and non-Christian Indians. Never have I been so intrigued by a people and an area as I have been by these Indians of the north — or so concerned. For some reason they have largely been forgotten by the Christian world.

In recent years there has been a resurgence of racial identity among the Indians and an increasing impatience with the injustices of the past and the subtle oppression of the present. Finally the voice of the Indian is beginning to make itself heard, and rightly so.

The stirring of racial pride, so long dormant, has brought a growing interest in a return to the old pagan ways, including a return to spirit worship. Some use the Indian religion cynically, as a means of stirring their brothers and uniting them for political power. Others go through the form without seriously considering what they do. Still others, and their numbers are increasing, embrace the evil spirits with their hearts.

The long-house ceremonies, the sun dance, and the choosing of spirits to worship are more than a series of quaint customs and interesting ways. They plunge deep into the world of satanic power and activity. That power is being manifested vividly in certain areas of the north today.

Whisper the Robin is the story of Marvin Lacendre, an intelligent young Cree who is caught in the struggle between spiritism and Christ.

WHISPER
THE
ROBIN

1

NINE-YEAR-OLD MARVIN played along the dock beside Birch Lake, waiting for the return of Jeremiah Rabbit Ear. His grandfather had left the Birch Lake Reserve in Northern Manitoba three days before to do his hunting and fishing, tirelessly paddling his canoe across the broad, flat waters of the lake.

While Marvin waited, he kept a wary eye on the decaying log shack some distance away where he lived with his mother and her current "friend." They had both come home two hours ago, drunk and fighting. Marvin had fled at the sound of their raised voices, knowing what would happen to him if he stayed.

He had never seen this Stanley "whatever-his-name-was" until a week ago. He was probably from Ile e la Cross or Deauval or Patuanak. His mother's friends came from many places, staying a few days or weeks, or even months if they happened to find special favor or had plenty of money and wine. Marvin accepted them the way he accepted the snow and rain that sifted through his thin jacket: stolidly, but with a certain caution. He had felt the anger of such men often enough to be wary of them all.

He ran a finger pensively across the bump that marred the bridge of his nose. He had gotten that for coming into the house when one of his mother's "husbands" wanted to be alone with her. The angered man had snatched a piece of stove wood from the box and had thrown it at Marvin, catching him full in the face.

His mother had pounced on the nearest weapon she could find, a long, razor-edged filleting knife, and drove the man out of the house. When he was gone, she had cradled her young son in her arms and cried until her tears mingled with his on his gaunt cheeks. Both of his eyes had been black for at least a month, and there was a bony knob on the side of his nose when it healed that would be with him the rest of his life.

The man who had broken his nose did not come back, but there were others, a continual procession of them. On several occasions when Marvin didn't have time to get out of the house before his mother's company arrived, he would dive under the bed and lay there, trembling, until the visitor left. If the fellow stayed too long, she usually tried to slip him some pemmican or a slab of smoked fish. Sometimes he got awfully hungry, but that was better than risking a beating.

As the time passed, Marvin tried to decide what he would do if his grandfather didn't get back for supper. He could go home with his friend James Rediron and get something to eat. In fact, he could even stay overnight at the Redirons'. As long as there was any food in the house, he would be welcome. That was the way of the Cree.

But even though he was welcome by custom at any home in the village, he would rather be with his grandfather, so he kept watching for that familiar canoe. It was still an hour before mealtime when a speck appeared on the horizon. It was so far away when he first saw it that he could scarcely be sure it was a canoe at all. It was only a blemish, a mole on the distant lip of the vast, mirrored lake.

The dark spot on the water moved closer, and was scarcely larger than a dragonfly on the calm water when he recognized it as belonging to his grandfather. A smile cracked the somber lines of his thin face.

He was the first to reach Rabbit Ear's canoe, running out into the water and grasping the bow with both hands.

"You got a moose!" he cried as he saw the canoe's heavy cargo.

Rabbit Ear climbed out of the canoe stiffly and, with the help of a dozen eager hands, hauled it up on shore.

"I went hunting for three weeks straight," one of the men said, "and I didn't even see a moose. Where did you get him, Jeremiah?"

"The Thunder gave him to me," he explained.

James Rediron snickered and Marvin glared at him. Nobody on the reserve paid much attention to the spirits any more, except some of the old ones who spent their days dreaming of the past. There were times when Marvin laughed at his grandfather himself, when the old man persisted in talking about tobacco and sweet grass and his spirit-helper who did everything for him, but that didn't give James cause to laugh at him.

Young Rediron saw the hostility in the other boy's eyes and cringed away. Marvin's fists tightened. Let that stupid James make one remark — just one — and he'd learn his lesson.

The men helped Jeremiah get the moose meat out of the canoe and up to the cabin where he lived alone.

"Come on in," he said as though it had just occurred to him to be generous. "I'll cut some off for you."

But they knew, as well as he, that it was custom that dictated his generosity. He had to share his good fortune with them lest his luck go sour and they withhold their meat from him.

He placed a hind quarter on the table and began to cut it carefully, giving each who helped him a large portion. They were the first to be served, but it did not end there. News spread that Jeremiah had killed a moose, and everyone in the village came to share it, or so it seemed. Even James Rediron appeared, a battered kettle in his grubby nine-year-old fist. Marvin glowered at him.

"What're you doing here?"

"My mom sent me for some meat."

Anger dusted the other boy's dark eyes. "You don't deserve any. You were laughing at him."

"I was only laughing about the Thunder that he said helped him to get his moose," James replied defensively. "You don't believe that yourself."

"I don't like it when you laugh at him, see?"

James sidled warily in the direction of the door, wondering whether it was safe for him to go inside where the meat was being distributed. Marvin decided it by backing away, and James darted inside.

When the hind quarter was gone, two men put up a front quarter without asking, and Jeremiah continued to slice, cheerfully joking with his friends. Towards the end the cuts got smaller, but there was some for everyone. When the last visitor left, Jeremiah had less than a hind quarter for himself.

But this did not disturb him. He sighed with immense satisfaction and turned to his grandson who was still lurking just outside the door.

"Go over and get your mother. Tell her I saved the best of the meat for her."

The boy did not move.

"Go!" Jeremiah's voice wore an edge. He was not used to being disobeyed.

Marvin shook his head uneasily. *"Kawin.* Stanley is there and — "

There was no need for Jeremiah to hear more. He knew his daughter.

"Kawin," he repeated, agreeing with the boy. "It is not good for you to go over there now. You stay with me tonight, eh?"

The ache in Jeremiah's belly grew as he thought about Betty and the bad things she was doing. No honorable woman would sport with any man in the village for a bottle of wine, or gamble, or quarrel and fight like an ugly-tempered she sled dog in harness. Her actions were enough to cause his head to bow in shame before the elders on the reserve.

If his wife had lived, he was sure Betty would have become a different person. She had been strong-willed, his wife, even in the last months before she died. *Ehe,* and she had been good in her living. The people still talked of her honorable ways and her kindness. She would have taken her daughter in hand.

Jeremiah had been disturbed about Betty as her dead mother would have been. At the first indication that he was going to have trouble with her, he built a house on an island two miles from the village and moved her there. She was only fourteen then, but she would sneak down to the lake on the opposite side of the island to wait for a lover in the canoe. Usually she was back in a few hours. But sometimes she would be gone for a week or more.

He had tried talking with her, but she wouldn't listen. He couldn't do anything with her. Now her own son couldn't stay at home for fear of her drunken friends. Jeremiah's humiliation was complete.

"We fix something to eat, Marvin," he said aloud. "We'll have a good piece of moose meat for our supper, eh?"

Already he was formulating a plan to approach his spirit-helper, the Thunder, about Betty. Where else could he turn?

The next day he gave the Thunder a piece of new cloth, taking it over to the sacred hill across the lake and spreading it on the bush halfway up the slope. Although it seemed to him that nobody cared about the spirits any more, especially the young men, few went near the hill and nobody climbed it. The steep, forbidden slope was the place where the Thunder-spirit kept his children.

Jeremiah wanted to take Marvin along, but decided against it. His grandson hadn't had the dream yet, and taking him to the hill might irritate the Thunder. The old man approached the hill with the proper respect, being careful not to disturb his spirit-helper, and spread out the two-yard length of cloth. Only then did he burn some sweet grass and tobacco to summon the Thunder so he could talk to him about the problems with Betty.

"And I would like to have your help when I go to her," he said, desperation creeping into his voice.

Betty and Marvin were sitting at the breakfast table that morning when Jeremiah got back from the hill and went to see her. Betty's face was still flushed and her eyes bloodshot from the drinking she had done. She got up as soon as her father came in and stood at the stove with her back to him, ashamed to face him.

"Marvin, go over and get some moose meat for your mother," he ordered presently. "I left it on the table."

Reluctantly the boy got to his feet, unwilling to leave when it seemed that something was going to be said that he ought to know about, yet hesitant to disobey his grandfather.

"Why didn't you bring it with you?" Betty asked uneasily.

"Marvin can get it."

The lad scampered away.

Once they were alone, she turned, crimson staining her dark cheeks. "Go ahead. Get it over with!"

He took a piece of smoked fish from the table and bit into it. That was the way it always was when he tried to talk to his daughter. She seemed to sense what he was about to say and made him feel like a fool.

Before he could speak, however, she coughed spasmodically; a dry, hacking cough that chilled his soul. It was the same cough her mother had had, and she had died of the sickness of the lungs.

"Why do you cough that way?" he demanded roughly, suddenly forgetting the purpose of his visit.

She shrugged and coughed again, spitting into a dirty scrap of cloth she took from the pocket of her slacks.

"Let me see that!"

She tried to throw the rag into the airtight heater, but he closed the gap between them with surprising speed and grabbed her wrist long enough to tear the bit of cloth from her bony fingers.

Her sputum was stained with blood.

"How long have you been coughing this way?" he persisted.

She was a little girl once more, squirming under the fire of his voice. "Not so long."

"One moon — two moons — three moons?"

"A — a couple of months, I guess."

"Why didn't you tell me?" He was angry now — even more angry than he had been over the bad way she was living.

Defiance glazed her blood-veined eyes. "I'm not goin' anywhere!"

The words ripped from him. "You go tomorrow!"

"You can't make me!"

"You go!"

16

The brief exertion was enough to start her coughing again until her strength was gone and she sank weakly to the bed. This time the sputum was bright scarlet.

"You stay in bed," he told her. "I'm going to see Beardy about getting someone to go to Deauval to radio for the plane."

With that he hurried out, her feeble protest following him.

Marvin and his grandfather stood along the shore with half the villagers, solemnly watching the floatplane taxi out into the lake. The people had seen this tableau repeated many times. There was not a family on the reserve that was untouched by tuberculosis. Usually the sick one returned after a year or so, only to have to go again when the stubborn ailment recurred. But there were times when one left, never to return. Although nobody mentioned that, it was what they all feared.

Marvin waved weakly as the aircraft roared down the lake and lifted clumsily into the air. He was still waving a lean arm when the plane disappeared over the trees. Only then did he turn, tremulously, to his grandfather.

"Why didn't you take care of her?" he wanted to know. "Why didn't you have your spirit-helper make her well so she wouldn't have to go away?"

The old man scowled. "The Thunder heals Indian sickness," he explained, "but this sickness of the lungs is white man's sickness. This the white man has to heal."

Touching the boy on the shoulder, he turned, trying to hide his own uneasiness, and made his way up the trail. Marvin walked beside him.

"Grandfather?"

Jeremiah did not answer.

"Grandfather?"

"Ehe?"

"She will come back, won't she?"

Jeremiah picked up a twig and snapped it in two.

"Won't she?"

2

THE NEXT MORNING Jeremiah got his rifle, grub sack, and blanket roll and took Marvin down to the canoe with him. He said nothing about the boy's mother going away, but the hurt was still gleaming mutely in his eyes. As usual, when he was troubled, he headed for the bush, away from the voices of those who did not feel his pain.

"We go hunting, I think," he said aloud.

Marvin squinted curiously at him. "But you just got a moose."

"We'll get another one maybe." There was a raw edge to his voice.

He didn't know why he was so short with Betty's only child the morning after she had been taken away. When he looked at the fatherless boy at his side, who might also be motherless before the snow fell again, the ache in his belly was like the pain of the sun dance when the thongs tore themselves free from the muscle and flesh.

The loneliness was bad enough for him, but the years that had stolen the strength from his legs and dimmed his eyes had also taught him to live with grief. Marvin was only a boy whose entire life stretched before him. And he knew nothing of sorrow.

Jeremiah rested a hand on his young grandson's shoulder. Why hadn't the sickness come to him, an old man, rather than his daughter? He had lived his life. He knew the despair of death, the numbing dread of watching his people stray from the old ways of tradition and honor. If only he could take his daughter's place and let her come back to the village to care for her son.

But, even if it were possible, he knew it would not be good. Betty was not like her mother. She had been lured from the safety of her people's ways just as a moose was teased from his muskeg fortress by the hunter's mating call. The things her mother hated had become a way of life for her. She could not raise her son to be a proud and stable heir to her family's honor, for she had no honor herself.

In spite of his years, Jeremiah knew that he could teach Marvin how to find his way in the bush, how to track a moose, and how to set a trap for the lynx and the beaver, that cautious builder of the north. He could teach him the ways of a Cree with the spirits, if Marvin would listen, making him a *shaman* who would be a force on the reserve because he could draw upon the power of the unseen world. He could mold his daughter's son into the sort of person he had always wanted her to be.

Perhaps this was the reason the spirits had given him the care of the boy. The thought brought strength to his tired legs and quickened his weary mind. There was still something he was good for; there was something he could do. Briefly a smile teased his lips.

The lessons for his grandson started immediately. There was pemmican and jerky in the canoe, but that was only because of the boy. He had brought food along in case they were stranded on an island in a high wind and there was nothing to eat. If he were alone, he could tighten his belt and close his mind to the lack of food, but he didn't want his grandson to know the growing ache of hunger in his belly. He would have to learn that some day before his education was complete, but not now. Not when the hurt of his mother's illness was so deep.

"Only the white man has to break his back under the load of food he carries into the bush," he told the boy. "Our people live off the country as they go. We travel light and fast."

"We brought grub along," Marvin reminded him.

"*Ehe,* but we're not going to eat it."

Marvin's gaze narrowed. It seemed strange to bring food with them and not use it, but there were times when there was no understanding his grandfather.

They made camp that night on the opposite shore, and the following morning Rabbit Ear took him out on the trail.

"Have you ever set a rabbit snare?"

"*Ehe.*"

Jeremiah was surprised. "You never catch any."

"But I know how to set a snare."

The old man laughed. "Today you will learn how to set a snare and *catch* rabbits."

Taking a length of steel wire, he made a snare quickly and fixed it across a rabbit run.

"See how it is done?"

Marvin wasn't quite sure how to make the loop the way his grandfather did or how to affix it in place, but he nodded that he did. He was afraid Jeremiah would not like it if he was slow to learn.

But his grandfather was patient. He handed the wire to Marvin.

"Show me."

Marvin's clumsy young fingers fumbled it into a crude loop.

"*Kawin.*" The graying Cree made him try again. "You do it this way so the loop closes easily over a rabbit's head or foot."

The first few times the boy failed miserably, but Jeremiah insisted that he keep at it until his strong young fingers formed the snares with ease. It was simple, then, to teach him where and how to set them.

He showed his grandson how to put out a net for fish and which berries were good to eat.

"Everybody knows about saskatoons and blueberries and raspberries," he said, "but sometimes it isn't so easy to find them."

Jeremiah showed him how to recognize wild cranberries and dewberries and rose hips. He taught Marvin how to catch grouse, spruce partridge, and squirrel.

And at night when they were sitting by the fire, he entertained and fascinated Marvin with stories of the spirits.

"And how did you get the Thunder to be your helper?"

20

Jeremiah squinted at him, approval gleaming in his eyes. Perhaps the boy was different than the other young ones in the village. Maybe he was going to be interested in the ways of his people.

"When I was only a little older than you are now," Jeremiah began. As he talked, he drifted back to that memorable time when he became a man by dreaming a dream and choosing his spirit-helper. "I went out into the bush alone. I made a nest in the highest tree I could find and stayed every night until the Thunder visited me and agreed to be my spirit."

Excitement widened Marvin's gleaming brown eyes. He had heard the story before, many times, but he loved every word of it.

"And why did you do that?"

"The Thunder is the most powerful spirit an Indian can get. It isn't every person he agrees to help."

"But you made up your mind that he was going to be your spirit, eh?"

The old man nodded. "I was going to get the Thunder to be my spirit if I had to stay in that tree every night until the leaves fell from the poplar."

"And he did!" the boy broke in triumphantly.

"That's right. He did." Jeremiah Rabbit Ear leaned back and closed his eyes, puffing thoughtfully on his pipe. There was much that he longed to tell his grandson about the spirit, but he would have to be careful not to give Marvin too much at one time. He had to build his interest, log by log, as a strong man builds his house. The boy had to have time enough to understand what he had been told before he was given more.

"The Thunder showed himself to me in a storm and told me he would be my spirit if I would agree to serve him."

"You made a deal with him," Marvin added.

"*Ehe,* I made a deal."

They talked, then, about serving the Thunder. Jeremiah explained how he could call his spirit by burning a little sweet grass and tobacco, and that he was expected to give him gifts.

" 'I like two yards of new cloth hung out in the bush,' the Thunder told me," the old man continued. "And if he does

21

something special for me, I'm supposed to give him something extra."

"But what if you ask him to do something and he doesn't do it?" the boy wanted to know. "What do you do then? Take away something that you gave him before?"

"Oh no!" Jeremiah's voice trembled lest his spirit hear what a terrible thing his grandson had said. "If the Thunder doesn't do something I ask him to do, it's because he's tired or sleeping, or he might be too busy right then. When that happens, I don't take a gift away from him. That would make him unhappy and he might do something bad to me. I give him more gifts." He raised his voice so if the Thunder happened to be listening he would know that Jeremiah had properly rebuked the boy.

Marvin didn't say anything, but he thought a lot about it afterwards. What use was it to have a spirit-helper if he was asleep or too busy when a fellow needed him?

They had been gone from the village almost two weeks but had not even seen a moose. That was not surprising to Jeremiah, nor did it disturb him. He had no real need for meat. His grub box was still filled with jerky and pemmican.

"Why don't you ask the Thunder to help?"

"I can't do that." His reply was quick. "I can't ask the Thunder to help me when we have plenty. If I should wake up his children or bother him when I don't need help, he might get mad at me." Fear glazed the old man's dark eyes. Marvin had to be warned about the spirits. They could not be trifled with. "That's one thing I learned long ago. A *shaman* has to treat his spirit-helper with respect."

Jeremiah went on to explain that it was one thing to summon the Thunder when his grub box and his belly were both empty. But he couldn't risk making his spirit angry by disturbing him when there was no need.

"It is good to have such a spirit as the thunder," he told Marvin as they paddled home. "He is the strongest of all the spirits. But he is also the most difficult to please, and he is the most apt to lose his temper."

Marvin decided right then that he didn't want to have anything to do with the Thunder. Having him for a spirit would be too scarey.

They could see the village on the distant hill when Marvin spoke of his mother for the first time since she had been taken out to the hospital.

"The mail comes today," he said. "Do you think maybe we'll have a letter from her?"

Jeremiah tried to smile, forcing it past the ugly dread that blocked its way. "A letter so soon? She will be too busy to write, I'm thinking."

The boy turned that over in his mind. He didn't like to talk about such things to his grandfather, but he had to ask.

"Do you think maybe she's somebody's adopted wife already?"

Jeremiah's thin lips tightened. A boy who was little taller than a canoe paddle should not think such things. He should not even know such things. In the old days he probably would have known about his mother and father; a one-room cabin offered little privacy. But he would not have known about other men taking a woman to be their adopted wife for as long or as short a time as the arrangement pleased them. And especially his own mother.

"No!" the old man exclaimed. "Your mother does not do that any more."

Marvin fell silent. In all the world there was no one like his grandfather. If he said that Marvin's mother wouldn't be the adopted wife of anyone, then it had to be true. Jeremiah did not lie.

A great sigh escaped the boy's lips. He wondered what it would be like not to be afraid of being clubbed or beaten by one of her drunken lovers.

There was no letter from Betty that week or the next or the next. A month passed after their return from the bush before they heard from her, a short note penciled with shaking fingers.

The old man studied the strange marks on the envelope, and for the second time in his life he wished he had done as his wife and daughter had and learned to read and write. The first time such a wish came to him had been when Betty's mother was taken

23

out to the sanatorium. He had had to get someone to read her letters to him then, as now.

"Here!" He thrust the envelope into the boy's hand. "Read it to me."

Marvin tried, but he had difficulty sounding out the words, and Jeremiah had to ask him to read the letter a second and yet a third time. He didn't know for sure what she meant by the things she wrote, but they didn't sound good. The doctors had been giving her some tests and now were talking about an operation.

Marvin looked up curiously. "What's an operation?"

Jeremiah scowled. "It's something to help your mother get well. Now go get a pail of water."

After the boy left, the old man held the envelope in his hand for half a minute or more. He'd have to go over to the Hudson Bay store and get Nils Laraviere to tell him about the operation. Nils would know about such things. Maybe it wasn't as terrible as he thought.

3

Fall came with its gay splashes of color in the bush; its cold rains and biting winds not stopping until the birds were driven south and the poplar, birch, and tamarack were whipped naked of their leafy clothes and left shivering in the first snows of winter.

It was a time of excitement and activity on the reserve. Men got their traps together and went out to wrest their living from the forests and streams in the way the Great Spirit intended the Cree to do. It was the winters that had kept Jeremiah's hopes for his people alive.

Jeremiah usually looked forward to the winter trapping with great anticipation, in spite of his years and the gnawing ache in his knees that made it increasingly difficult for him to get about on snowshoes.

But this year as the others got ready for the trap line, a vague uneasiness stirred within Jeremiah. For the first time since he had taken the rites and vows and become a man, he lacked the stomach for the bush. It was almost as though he didn't care any more.

One problem was that Marvin was living with him. Of course he could take the boy out of school to go trapping. There were those who did, reasoning that the lessons of the bush were better for their sons than those of the white man's books, and Jeremiah agreed with them. The time to learn the way of the beaver, the mink, and the squirrel was when a lad was young. But Laraviere advised him to leave Marvin in school. The Hudson Bay mana-

25

ger was Jeremiah's friend, and he was wise in the ways of men. Jeremiah trusted him and valued his advice.

Laraviere had been the one who read Betty's letter and told him what the operation was.

"There is something inside of her that the doctor thinks is bad for her," he explained, scanning the letter again. "They want to put her to sleep and cut out the bad thing so she'll get better and be able to come back to the reserve."

The old man thought about that. "I don't think I like it, this operation," he said.

"It isn't anything to get so upset about." Nils understood the concerned father's uneasiness and tried to find words to give him confidence that his daughter was going to be all right. "The doctors do it all the time."

"When the doctors put them to sleep," he said, "does it ever happen that they do not wake up?"

Laraviere's gaze found his. He had never lied to his friend; he could not start now. "It does happen, Jeremiah," he admitted.

A sudden chill skittered up the old man's spine. "Then it is not good," he announced. "It is not good to have this — this operation."

"It happens, Jeremiah," Laraviere said. "I wouldn't lie to you by saying it doesn't, but it's still better for her. The doctors must think Betty has to be cut open in order to get well."

Jeremiah shook his head stubbornly. "It is not good."

"I know just how you feel, but if she were my own daughter, I'd want her to have the operation."

This surprised Rabbit Ear. He had never heard his friend so insistent. "You would?"

"I would." He eased his portly frame out of the chair and waddled over to where Jeremiah was standing. "Betty is almost like my own daughter. I wouldn't tell you that I think she ought to have the operation if I didn't believe it."

The graying Indian paused. Betty had been a little girl when the Frenchman came to the reserve to manage the store. And when she got older, she had thrown herself at him shamelessly. A lesser man would have gone off into the bush with her, but not Laraviere. He gave her a good scolding and told her she couldn't come to the store if she acted that way again. From then on Jeremiah knew Laraviere was a true friend of his and of the Cree.

Jeremiah had already made up his mind about the operation, however. They might cut his daughter open — it didn't occur to him to protest — but he was against it.

Another letter came from Betty just before freeze-up stopped the floatplanes. Laraviere read it to him twice, wincing at the news he had to reveal to his old friend. She wasn't feeling any better, she wrote. The doctors still hadn't decided when to operate. They wanted to build up her strength first.

Jeremiah was grateful for the news that they would not do this — this cutting on her yet, but the letter gave him an aching in the heart.

"Maybe she writes so because she's lonesome," Laraviere told him, trying to find something to hang his hope on.

Jeremiah shook his head. It was not like Betty. Wherever she was, she made friends. That was one of her problems. She made too many of the wrong kind of friends.

"Maybe you should go see her," Laraviere suggested.

"Me?" His eyes widened. "I don't have any money except for a little grub and the clothes Marvin needs. I don't have enough to go anywhere."

"I have a little."

The old man thought about making the trip. It would be good to see Betty once again; to look into her eyes himself and see whether she was as sick as he feared she was. It was like Laraviere to offer to pay for the trip. The big man's skin was white, but Jeremiah had always been sure that he had the heart of a Cree.

Still, he felt that he couldn't go. He tried to make himself believe that he had to stay home because of Marvin, but that was only an excuse. He could knock at any door on the reserve and find a place where the boy could stay while he was gone. Laraviere would take him, too.

Actually, Jeremiah refused to go because he was afraid. He

had never been in the cities of the south, like Saskatoon where the sanatorium was, but he had heard much about them. From the stories that came back to the reserve, he knew they were frightening places with cars dashing noisily everywhere and belching smoke that hurt the lungs. And they were clogged with people, hurrying as though they had a big fat beaver in a trap and were afraid someone would steal it from them before they could get to it.

And the planes at the airport! They said some of them were big enough to hold all the people on the reserve. Just one of them could swallow the twin-engine Canso that brought in supplies for the Bay and still be hungry. No, he could never go to a place like that.

Marvin seldom asked about his mother any more, although his grandfather could read the concern in the boy's eyes. And he wrote to her every week, whether he heard from her or not.

Betty answered her son occasionally, a few shaking lines scrawled on cheap notepaper.

Jeremiah tried to avoid the subject of his daughter as much as possible, shoving it to the far reaches of his mind and pretending she was just away. Only he couldn't avoid thinking of the dread reality of her illness.

He wished he had a badger so he could look in its blood and tell what was going to happen. He had never seen a badger himself, but his grandfather had told him about the powers of the prairie animal when he was a boy.

There was nothing better than badger blood to tell a man of his future. But there was no use thinking about badger blood. They were too far north for the prairie animal.

He could burn some sweet grass and tobacco and talk to the Thunder about Betty. Even though it was white man's sickness, the spirit-helper might be able to tell what was going to happen to her. Or he could look into the eyes of an animal or the side of a polished ax head. But, somehow, he didn't feel free to do any of those things. And a man had to be sure he was doing what he should or the spirits would get angry and he would accomplish nothing.

Jeremiah wasn't sure when he thought of doing the shaking tipi, or why he hadn't thought of it before. It was the best means a *shaman* had of divining the future.

He went to talk with Chief Beardy about it. The chief didn't have a spirit-helper of his own, but he was wise in the ways of the beings of the other world. He sat cross-legged on the grass near his house, tugging at his pipe. A matter as serious as the conjuring lodge was not to be decided quickly or without deliberation.

"It might not work, Jeremiah," he reminded his old friend. "And you know what that would mean?"

"*Ehe.* That I would die soon."

Beardy closed his eyes. No one on the reserve could remember how long it had been since the shaking tipi had been done. Many of the younger ones would not even know what it was. But it would be exciting to have it again.

"I think it is good, Jeremiah."

The old man nodded sagely. He had already reached that decision himself, but it was good to know the chief agreed.

As with everything else he did, Jeremiah planned the shaking tipi with care. It would be held at the time of the new moon. He would go out into the bush alone to cut the six poles he needed, and they would be heavy, as large as a man's forearm and almost ten feet long. They would be properly placed, as it was important that the birch, tamarack, and poplar be alternated. The order didn't matter as long as he didn't have tamarack against tamarack or poplar against poplar. The new moon was his own innovation. Knowing his spirit-helper, it seemed better to hold the event at the time of the new moon when the spirits were more active.

He chose the place for the tipi, a prominent spot not far from his cabin, with plenty of room for the people to gather around it.

The day before the conjuring ceremony Jeremiah brought in the poles and the moose hides. A dozen men offered their services, but he refused them all. That morning as he set out for the bush to cut the poles, he would not even allow Marvin to accompany him. It would have been good to let his grandson see the care one had to use in dealing with his spirit-helper, but Marvin hadn't yet had a dream so he would be unacceptable to the Thunder.

"You stay here," Jeremiah ordered, "and if anyone asks where I've gone, tell them I'm getting the poles."

The boy didn't like having to stay in the village. "George Beardy says other medicine men let someone help them build the lodge."

Painfully Jeremiah pulled himself erect. "I am the one who is having the conjuring tent. I decide who prepares for the tent and who builds it!"

He went out into the bush, his ax over his shoulder, and came in before noon dragging six carefully chosen poles. He dug the holes for them himself, a generous two feet deep, and securely tamped the poles in place to form a rough circle five or six feet in diameter.

"Those poles are too heavy, Jeremiah," one of the younger men joked. "You'll never be able to shake them."

"It is for those like you that I chose heavy poles. When you see them move tonight, you'll know it is the spirits and not Jeremiah you are seeing at work."

The speaker fell silent. He had scoffed at the shaking tipi, but his scorn had a hollow, empty sound — the rattling of small stones in a can.

Once the old man had the poles securely placed, he took the larger of the two willow hoops he had fashioned and put it in place on the inside, some three or four feet above the ground. The smaller hoop, also made of two willow poles, was put over the top on the outside of the heavy poles that made up the conjuring tent.

Jeremiah laid green boughs inside on the ground and carefully draped the moose hides about the poles to form the tipi. Then he tied two small bells to the top of the tent where the poles came together.

Several of the older men kept the dogs and the small children away. Let a dog lift his leg at one of the poles and it was desecrated beyond use. Likewise small children playing around the tipi without understanding its sacred import could kindle the anger of the spirits. The men chased James Rediron and several of his curious friends away and would have kept Marvin from the tipi as well, but Jeremiah ordered them to let him remain.

The boy's friends watched enviously from a distance, but he pretended not to know that they were there. Now let that James Rediron laugh at his grandfather!

That night when Marvin and Jeremiah were in their cabin eating bannock and smoked fish while others guarded the newly constructed conjuring lodge, he tried to find out more about it.

"Will the spirits be in the tent with you?" Awe shook his young voice.

"*Ehe.*"

"W-Won't you be scared?"

"Scared?" Jeremiah's thin cackle broke the silence. "The spirits are my friends."

Marvin relaxed; his grandfather's lack of anger made him even bolder. "Will the Thunder be there?"

"*Ehe,*" he said, as though the sound of his voice would give him more strength to summon the spirit. "The Thunder will be there."

"And you will ask him if my mother is going to get well and come home?"

The old man's eyes clouded.

4

JEREMIAH HAD BEEN so concerned about his own problems that he was completely unprepared for the interest the others on the reserve were taking in the conjuring tent or for the questions they wanted answered.

"Here is a pound of tobacco," one man said, keeping his voice down so no one else would hear him. "Ask the spirits if my wife has a lover."

A little later another came with a tin of lard and some smoked fish. "Find out if I will do well with my nets this year."

There were others, too, just like in the old days when he had the shaking tipi. And there would be more after he went into the tent and the ceremony started.

Jeremiah tingled with excitement. *Ehe,* it was going to be like the old days. Only Betty and the dread sickness of the lungs that threatened to steal her from him and Marvin kept him from tasting every moment with enjoyment.

Jeremiah would have told no one, but the night before the conjuring lodge he did not sleep. It was not a small thing he was proposing in trying to conjure before the entire reserve. He was getting old. Although he could still summon the Thunder to help him with trapping or hunting or ordinary problems, the shaking tipi required strong powers. What if his power to call up the spirits had diminished, even as the strength in his once powerful body had begun to fade?

The next day Jeremiah kept to the house, not even going out

to relieve himself. His own silence was marred by Marvin's excitement-loosed tongue. He wished the boy would go out and play with his friends, but that was too much to expect with the anticipation of the shaking tipi. As the afternoon wore on, his grandson scarcely moved from the window.

"Look, grandfather, the people are already gathering around the conjuring tent."

At this point that only increased the old man's apprehension.

"Aren't you proud?"

Jeremiah snorted.

"I am. I'm proud that you're my grandfather."

"Go get a pail of water."

The boy groaned.

"Be quick about it."

"You always make me go after water," he grumbled.

Nevertheless, Marvin picked up the pail and started for the door. By the time he returned from the lake with the bucket brimming, the tent was completely encircled. The men were in the front rows and the women and children were behind, usually as curious as the male members of the reserve, but more timid and afraid.

Shortly after sundown, before the great moon pushed out of the celestial seas and hung its orange lantern above the horizon, Jeremiah stirred himself. Getting painfully to his feet, he went into the cabin's lone bedroom, stripped to his loincloth, and wrapped his gaunt torso in a blanket.

"Come, Marvin, they are waiting for us." He shuffled across the rough pine floor and out the cabin door. "Come."

The boy jumped to his feet and hurried after him, strutting proudly a pace or two behind. He was abreast of the women and children who fringed the circle of men and older boys when a pair of bold young eyes caught his gaze. Marvin stared at the girl, awed for an instant by the beauty of her dark face and long black hair.

Marvin didn't know who she was. He had never seen her before, but he figured she must be younger than he was.

James Rediron and several of the boys his own age were standing nearby watching him and his grandfather, new respect in their eyes.

The people moved quickly to make a corridor for Jeremiah and his grandson. Marvin's friends motioned for him to stand by them, but he went on to the front row where he stood beside George Beardy.

Jeremiah circled the tent, inspecting it carefully to be sure all was in order. Then he paused, his hand on the flap, and for the first time allowed himself a glance at the people.

Chief Beardy stepped forward holding out a small pillow for the old man to kneel on inside, one small concession to his aching bones. Slowly Jeremiah advanced to meet his friend and chief, took the pillow with a quick movement, and pivoted without even looking at his grandson. He ducked inside the conjuring tent and closed the moose hide flap after him.

Silence blanketed the tense knot of people that had gathered about the tipi, choking off the hushed babble of many voices. Even the young and arrogant who professed to scorn the old ways laughed no more. They, too, were caught up in the emotion of the moment, carried back to the time before the white man came when all the Cree nation worshiped the spirits and looked to the conjurers with their shaking tipis, badger blood, and animal eyes to foretell the future.

Someone in the crowd stirred and coughed nervously, and then all was silent.

Marvin, standing beside the village chief, stared at the tent, his face the color of ashes and his hands trembling. The spirits were going to be inside with only a thickness of moose hide between him and them.

He should have stayed with James and Marcel, keeping some distance between himself and the spirits. But, approaching the tipi proudly with his grandfather, he had wanted to get as close as he could. Now, however, as the flap moved back into place to hide his grandfather from view, he fought against the sudden compulsion to flee.

That would never do! He didn't know much about the spirits, but his grandfather had taught him enough so he knew that if he left, he might cause them to get so angry they would come after him themselves. The Thunder might whisk him away to that sacred hill where he kept his children and never let him go free again, or the spirit might do something terrible to his grandfather. No, regardless of what happened, Marvin had to stay.

After what seemed to be an interminable period of time, the top of the conjuring lodge began to move slowly. At first the people could not be sure it had moved at all, the movement was so slight. For a moment it stopped, gathering strength. Then, with a thin, rustling noise and the faint tinkle of the bells in the top of the tent, it moved once more.

An awed gasp went up from the crowd.

While they stared, the top of the tent lurched violently in an arc the length of a tall man's arm. The bells clattered as the tempo increased, and the people, struck dumb by the manifestation, began to sway in rhythm to the erratic gyrations.

The tense hush was shattered by the weird, singsong chant of the conjurer that rose and fell with the movement of the tipi. Then Jeremiah's voice seemed to change, taking on deep bass tones and a new resonance, until even Marvin could note no resemblance to his grandfather's voice.

The boy shuddered. From inside the tipi a loon called, followed by the quick, nervous barking of a fox and the familiar prattle of a whiskey jack. A wolf growled, and a song sparrow sounded his shrill obbligato above the other animal voices.

Marvin gulped noisily and George Beardy looked down at him, disapproval darkening his wrinkled face.

"Waaci," a strange voice from inside the tent said suddenly.

A great sighing sound went up from the crowd.

"Shake hands. Shake hands."

The old man's thin, cackling laugh sounded loud and clear above the muffled noises in the tent.

"Who asked you to come here?"

"This is the place where you have your poles. I came to cheer you up. I like the place where you built my home."

"I built it so everybody could see."

"It is good. I shake hands with all the women who came here tonight. I shake hands with the men."

Marvin saw a great bumping against the moose hides from inside the tent, as though someone was hitting them with a powerful fist. He moistened his parched lips and grasped Beardy's rough hand with his own moist fingers.

"Who's in there talking with my grandfather?" he asked, his voice sounding strangely harsh in the still air.

"That's his *Mistabeo,* the Thunder spirit."

A convulsive shudder racked the boy's thin shoulders. Maybe he would never see his grandfather again.

At that moment another voice came from within the tent, a high-pitched singing voice like a woman chanting. *"Waaci.* Greetings. Shake hands. I came to see the tent he made for you. It is a good tent."

"Ehe, it is a good tent. He remembered to make it right. I'm pleased with the poles he made for me."

"Then get busy," Jeremiah broke in, teasing. "Tell me what I want to know."

"About the wife of the man who came to you? She's out in the bush with her lover right now."

Laughter swept nervously across the crowd.

Marvin was surprised they could hear the voices of the spirits so clearly and understand them so well. He had thought only his grandfather would be able to hear what the spirits told him.

"What about my fur?" a tall, angular Cree called out. "Who stole from me last winter?"

"He was not from this reserve."

The voice faded until it was all but indistinguishable.

"What?" the people asked. "Speak up. Speak up!"

The spirit gave a name, and the trapper swore savagely. "My own brother-in-law."

Now the questions were coming from all sides of the conjuring lodge. For a time the spirit answered them, but at last he spoke gruffly.

"Enough! The one who built this house for me has questions of his own to ask. He has pleased me with the house he built for me. He was careful to build it right. Now it is time for him to ask questions of his own."

The crowd fell silent, hushed by the stern voice.

"You want to know about your daughter, *kawin?*"

"*Ehe.* She is at the white man's place for treating the sickness of the lungs. When will she come home?"

"It won't be for many moons."

That seemed to disturb Jeremiah. He coughed nervously.

"W-will she get well?"

Again the hush was drawn taut with emotion.

Jeremiah repeated his question.

"You ask hard things."

"Not too hard for you."

The answer was unintelligible to the crowd outside. "What? What?"

The fury of the shaking and the muffling gabble of animal voices continued, but no one outside was able to distinguish anything the Thunder spirit said. Even Jeremiah's voice was indecipherable. It was several minutes before the spirit's voice sounded loud and clear again.

"But you will live to see your grandson become a man and arrange a sun dance in honor of his spirit-helper."

Presently the tipi stopped shaking as the animal sounds died away. Some time later the old man pushed back the moose hide flap and stepped out, his bronzed face inscrutable in the light of the big moon. Marvin ran up to him.

"What did he say, grandfather? What did he say about my mother? Will she get well?"

Jeremiah's voice was weary. "We'll talk about that when we get home."

Even before Jeremiah started up to his house with his grandson, Beardy and several others began to dismantle the conjuring lodge. They did not stop until they had completely taken it apart and put the pieces away. Such was the proper treatment for the shaking tipi once the conjurer had finished with it.

Marvin followed Jeremiah into the cabin and turned mutely to close the heavy plank door. There was no need for him to ask the question again. He already knew the answer; it was written in his grandfather's haunted, grief-lined face.

The old man shuffled into the other room and sagged wearily to the bed, his strength spent by the ordeal just ended. Marvin stood uneasily at the bedroom door, looking in at the frail form.

The color that usually mounted high in the boy's cheeks was gone, pulled slowly away by the events of the last hour. His lips were straight and as taut as drawn wire in an effort that almost succeeded in keeping them from trembling. His bony figure was that of a boy, but his soft brown eyes, more accustomed to laughter than sorrow, were suddenly old, as though they had seen and understood too much, too soon.

He was expected to crawl in on the other side of the bed with his grandfather. Usually they would lie for a time talking about the old days when the Cree stood tall and proud, a people to be feared.

But not tonight.

His mother would not be coming back — not now or ever. That realization churned ceaselessly through Marvin's being. That had been the Thunder's message to his grandfather in the shaking tipi. The spirit had not caused it to happen, nor could he prevent it from happening. Like his grandfather said, the sickness of the lungs was a white man's disease. It took the white man's medicine to heal it.

Sitting in the darkness the boy could still see his mother's haggard face as she swept him into her arms. He could still feel the warmth of her tears as she crushed her cheek against his. He could still hear her dry, hacking cough and see the hurt in her dark-circled eyes. At times these memories had awakened him in the small, silent hours of the night when his grandfather was snoring quietly. And he would lay there until the morning, with the hurt and loneliness so great he thought he could not bear them. Now it was even worse. He knew he would never see his mother again.

Scalding tears clung for an instant to his long, black lashes before burning their way down his dark cheeks. Silently he sobbed, shoulders shaking.

38

Towards morning Marvin slept, resting his head against his arms on the table. When Jeremiah awoke, he found him there, exhaustion mercifully bringing rest. The old man stood beside his grandson momentarily, his bony fingers lightly stroking the boy's head.

Jeremiah had not slept much either, disturbed as he was by the message from the Thunder. He had been dreading the ordeal of telling the boy about his mother, but now he saw that there was no need to tell him. Marvin already knew.

The sound of the floatplane awakened the boy.

"Someone is coming, grandfather." Hope gleamed in the boy's almond eyes. "Do you suppose it could be mother?"

"*Kawin.*" There was no need to give him hope again. It would only make the hurt greater when the news came.

Even as he spoke, Marvin glimpsed at the insignia on the wing. "The RCMP! Why are they coming here?"

Jeremiah went to the door uneasily. The Mounties only came when there was trouble. The sight of that plane brought concern to everyone.

"Why do they come here, grandfather?" Marvin demanded.

Jeremiah shrugged. Why did the white man do a lot of things? There had been a time when the Cree had had their own laws; when the chief and his council ruled their people with occasional help from the medicine man. But no more. Now it was the white man who came swooping in to snatch someone away. It brought anger and humiliation to all of them, but what could they do?

"I hate those Mounties!" Marvin blurted, emotion contorting his young face.

Jeremiah shook his head. It was not good for the boy to hate. It would only cause trouble later. The day of the Cree had passed. It could not be brought back.

His lips parted to chide his grandson, but he could not. There would be time for that later, after the hurt about his mother had begun to ease.

"I'm going down and see what they want," the boy exclaimed. "Okay?"

"You do that. Then come back and tell me." It could be that the Mounties had heard about the conjuring lodge and were there to take him to jail. He didn't think it was against their laws, but there was no knowing what stupid regulations they would make.

It was half an hour later before Marvin sped back to the cabin and burst through the door. "Grandfather!"

The old man stirred. *"Ehe?"*

"They came to take Emil Bear to jail!"

Jeremiah's forehead crinkled. "Did they catch him bootlegging?"

"Kawin. It was for beating his wife. Laraviere sent someone to Deauval to radio for them. They're taking her to the hospital in Prince Albert.

Fear ripped through Jeremiah's twisted body. Emil was the one who had asked him to find out from the spirits if his wife had a lover.

He hoped the RCMP didn't learn about the shaking tipi and the part he and the Thunder had had in getting the information for Emil that had caused him to beat his wife. The white man didn't understand such things. They would take him off to jail just when Marvin needed him the most.

"Are they asking about me?"

His grandson shook his head.

"Do they know about the conjuring lodge?"

"Kawin." The boy shook his head. "Nobody told him anything."

Jeremiah nodded. He should have known it would be that way. The only one in the village who might have told them was Laraviere, and he hadn't been at the tipi last night. Wearily he grasped the table with his hands and, unhinging his arthritic knees, he lowered himself painfully to the fish box chair.

5

When Aldina Brouilette saw Marvin coming down the hill the afternoon following the conjuring lodge, she left her friends and walked toward him.

"Come on, Aldina," one of them called after her. "It's your turn."

"I don't want to play any more."

She pulled her ebony braids forward over her shoulders and waited for him on the path.

"Hello." Her smile invited him to stop.

Marvin looked at her. She was the same girl who had smiled at him the night before.

"Oh, hi."

"I saw you last night at the shaking tipi."

"*Ehe.* I was there." The memory stabbed through him. He would never be able to forget the violently gyrating tipi or the horror of the Thunder's message about his mother.

"Your grandfather was the one who did it."

"*Ehe.*" He was twisting uneasily, trying to see if Marcel or Velmer or James were around to see him. They would never forget it if they saw him talking to a girl.

"Weren't you proud?"

"I guess so." He kicked the dirt with a scuffed moccasin, wishing he could get away from her before he was seen.

"I would be," she told him.

"I've got to go now."

Her dark young face clouded. "You haven't even asked me what my name is or why we came here."

Desperation crept into his eyes and he sidled past her.

"I — I've got to go."

"My name's Aldina Brouilette, and we came to visit my sister." Tears trembled on her eyelashes. "And I don't even *care* what your name is." With that she whirled and fled.

Grateful for his reprieve, Marvin hurried down the path.

During the next few weeks it seemed to him he saw Aldina everywhere he went. She was in the store when he went to get tobacco or flour for his grandfather; she was on the dock when he and the guys were waiting for the Canso to come in with supplies. And when they played baseball, she was watching nearby.

"What's *she* doing out here?" he asked Velmer, as though he didn't know.

His friend scowled. "Search me."

James Rediron approached the store cautiously, his dark eyes gleaming. Laraviere had ordered him out and told him he could not come back the last time when he had caught him stealing. But nobody was afraid of the old Frenchman. He stormed around and swore like everything when he got mad, but it didn't last long. And when it was over, he forgot everything he had said.

Besides, James' empty belly ached. For the past three days his aunt had been away and he had been scrounging for food. He could have gone to Velmer's or Daniel's or even to Marvin's grandfather, but fishing hadn't been good and nobody had killed a moose in weeks. All the people had to eat was macaroni and bannock.

It had been a little better before his mother met that Chipewyan from Uranium City and ran off with him. She had left him alone and locked out of the house occasionally, the same as her sister did, but it hadn't happened as often and she hadn't stayed away as long.

But that didn't help him now. He had to get in the store and find something to eat — a couple of candy bars or a box of cookies or anything else he could grab.

Hesitantly James made his way up the wooden steps and tugged the door open. The bulbous storekeeper was leaning against the counter, his little round eyes cold and staring.

"*Waaci,*" James said, pinning on his best smile. "Greetings."

"I thought I told you to stay out of here!"

"I — I — "

"Then git! I ain't havin' no thief around!"

"But — "

"You'll wind up in jail one of these days if you keep picking up everything you see. D'you hear?"

James backed towards the door, his lips trembling. A tear eased out of the corner of his eye and moved silently down his cheek.

Laraviere saw it.

"Just a minute!" He waddled towards James. "You stay right there!"

"But I ain't done nothin'!"

"Nobody says you have — today." The big Frenchman stared intently at him, his fat face as emotionless as a beaver's. "That aunt of yours still gone?"

"*Ehe.*" The word trembled out. He didn't know what that could have to do with Laraviere, but it must mean something bad to have him act that way. He had to get away if he could.

James backed away, but Laraviere grabbed him roughly by the arm. "That's what I thought. That's just about what I thought. And who've you been living with since she's been gone?"

"N-N-Nobody." He struggled to free himself, but those strong fingers only clamped tighter.

"Where'd you sleep last night?"

"In Morin's old shed."

"That's about what I figured, too. Come on." He turned, shoving the boy ahead of him.

Panic leaped to James Rediron's eyes. "Where're you taking me?"

"To the back room to fix you something to eat. I can't have

43

anybody going hungry around here." The softness that came briefly left his eyes. "It's bad for business."

That night Laraviere put James to bed in the guest room after the biggest meal the boy had ever eaten.

"You'll probably steal half of what I've got before morning," he grumbled, "but I've got to get my rest. I don't want to lay awake half the night worrying about you trying to sleep in that old shed."

James Rediron stayed with Laraviere until his aunt came back the last of the week. It was the best three days he could remember. He had told himself he wasn't going to steal from the burly Frenchman again, but when he left the house that last day he saw a new filleting knife on the kitchen table near the sink. Impulsively he edged to the cabinet and hid the knife under his sweater.

Marvin saw James on the dock in front of the store later that afternoon and asked him about his staying with Laraviere.

"He told me that I can come and stay with him any time," he boasted.

"He did?" Marvin was curious. "The last I heard, he wasn't going to let you in the store again."

"Who told you that?" James blustered.

"He told me so himself."

James Rediron's cheeks were a flaming scarlet. "That's not true."

"Go in and ask him, if you don't believe me. Just go in and ask him if he didn't tell grandfather and me that he wasn't going to let you come in the store any more because you've swiped so much stuff from him."

"He was just joking about that," James muttered lamely.

Marvin couldn't understand why Laraviere would let James stay at his house. It sure didn't make sense — especially when the old Frenchman talked with him a second time about James.

"Don't you run around with that young scamp, Marvin. Don't have anything to do with him."

"Why not?" he asked.

The big man's broad features darkened. "Because he's bad medicine, that's why."

"What's he done?"

Laraviere's patience exploded. "You just never mind what he's done, boy. He's no good for you or any other nice boy. If you want to stay out of trouble, you'll stay plumb away from him, y'hear?"

Marvin figured that James was still stealing from the store, but that didn't help him understand why the Frenchman took him into his house while his aunt was away.

Marvin spent most of the rest of the summer fishing with his grandfather and camping in the bush. Two weeks after the shaking tipi Jeremiah had him helping run the nets.

Marvin was an apt pupil. He soon knew exactly where to place the nets for the higher-priced whites and yellows; he could mend a net with deft, sure knots and could string floats or weights with ease. Like any other Cree boy or man, he didn't like to gut or fillet fish, but he could do it as well as anyone if it was necessary. And he could paddle a canoe or handle a kicker as well as any boy his age.

"*Ehe*," Jeremiah murmured expansively as they sat by their campfire, the thin corkscrew of smoke working its way upward in the still air. "You are doing well, Marvin. As well as any other ten-year-old in the village."

"James Rediron doesn't even know how to put out a net" Marvin muttered. He dared not contradict his grandfather, but by inference he could remind the old man that he knew more about the bush than most of his friends. "And he's never made a rabbit snare or caught a squirrel in his life. And he doesn't know *anything* about cutting up a moose."

"*Ehe*, that is true, but James doesn't have a father or a grandfather to teach him, Marvin."

He thought about that. Maybe it explained something else. "Is that why Laraviere took him in while his aunt was away?"

Jeremiah tapped the ashes from his cold pipe with the heel of his hand. *"Ehe.* That is the reason. It is hard for a boy like James. Don't ever forget that."

Marvin nodded seriously. He knew it was hard for James Red-iron, but it was hard for him, too. It wouldn't be long until he wouldn't even have a mother.

Jeremiah talked much with his grandson during the next few weeks, trying to teach him everything he ought to know about the harsh land in which they lived. But there was one subject that was closed between them; constantly in mind, but shut off as though there were no words to express the torment that they both felt.

Marvin tried to forget about that terrible night when Jeremiah had summoned his spirit-helper. He pretended that it had never happened at all, that his mother was just away and would be coming back soon. And when she did come back, everything was going to be different.

Frequently he closed his eyes and imagined he could see her bright face through the window of the floatplane as it taxied up to the dock. He could hear her lilting voice and feel the warmth of her arms as they enveloped him and drew him close.

He saw himself in the house with her when the men came around, one by one, wanting to stay for supper and the night. Some of them had bottles and some had money and pretty clothes for her. But she wouldn't have anything to do with them, and Marvin was happier than he had ever been.

Then reality would stab through the joyous vapor of his dreams.

6

ALDINA BROUILETTE SAT cross-legged on the ground between her mother and older sister, one hand tightly grasping the green hide on which they were working. Mary Brouilette glanced proudly at her youngest daughter. She had the same distinctive, delicate features; the same smooth, unblemished skin the color of freshly smoke-tanned hide; and the same eyes that danced with excitement when she talked, especially if boys were present. In a few years she also would have her mother's provocative figure. Although Mary would not admit it, Aldina was her favorite daughter.

"How do I do it?" Aldina asked aloud, her eyes fixed on her just-married sister.

"You must hold the scraper so," Florence told her, newly acquired patience for this girl-child in her voice. "And see that you get all the fat and meat off the hide."

Although Aldina was still a child, she already knew much that women of the tribe were expected to know by the time they were married. She was learning to make jerky and pemmican and for the past few months had been smoking fish and mending nets. Mary taught her how to make trap sets for mink and beaver and how to put out snares to catch rabbits or squirrels. She had not planned to teach her to do bead work for a year or two, but Florence, in a burst of sisterly love, had taken over that responsibility.

She gave Aldina some beads from a pair of worn-out moccasins and taught her to affix them to a piece of cloth with ordinary thread. Soon her deft fingers were creating designs as intricate as anything Florence could make.

"Look, mother," the older girl exclaimed, holding up her sister's latest effort. "Isn't that beautiful?"

"Hmmm," Mary murmured in agreement. Aldina would be an example to the younger girls in the village and a pride to her mother. It would be a day to remember when the people sought out her daughter to tan their moose hides or make their beaded jackets and moccasins.

Aldina helped her mother and sister with the fresh moose hide until the last traces of fat were scraped away and it was ready for stretching to dry on poles high enough to keep it out of reach of the always-hungry dogs. Then she scooted off to join her friends.

That was the summer the pert, red-haired missionary came to the reserve. From the first time she gathered the women and children about her to tell stories on the cloth-covered board, Aldina adored her.

Miss Emily Bannister talked about strange things that few of the people had ever heard. Only one old woman could remember a white man who had come to live among them years ago. He had talked about such things, and some of the people had even helped him build a little church, on the edge of the village. But when he got sick and had to leave, they no longer used the church, and in a year or two nobody remembered much of what he had said.

Aldina was intrigued by the missionary's fiery hair and the freckles splotched across her saucy nose. She had never seen freckles before and was fascinated by them. She would hunker on a chair near the table in Emily's two-room cabin and listen to her talk about Jesus.

The Indian girl had never heard such a thrilling story. Emily said God became man and lived on earth, but the people didn't know who He was and killed Him. They nailed Him to a tree until He was dead — at least it looked something like a tree to Aldina.

Tears came to Miss Emily's eyes when she talked about it and to Aldina's as she listened.

Her hand went up quickly. "Was He still God, Miss Emily?"

"*Ehe*. He was still God. He was man, too, but He was still God."

"Then why didn't He come down from there and kill them all?" Aldina's brown eyes flashed and anger flecked her young voice.

The missionary took a step or two forward. "I used to wonder about that myself. He could have done it, but He had a reason for dying on the cross. He did it so you and I can have our sins forgiven. And when we put our trust in Him, we can go to Heaven."

Aldina thought she wanted to become a Christian like Miss Emily, but there was so much she didn't understand.

She was the one who first talked with Marvin about Miss Emily. She waited for him on the path again and asked him to go to the missionary's house.

"You'd like it," she said. "Miss Emily tells stories and everything."

"It's for women and girls and little kids."

Aldina hesitated. "She might talk to God about your mother, if you asked her."

"A lot of good that'd do," he snorted.

But the more he thought about what she'd said, the more he wondered if maybe the missionary could help. He lay awake half the night thinking about it.

He would have gone to talk to Miss Emily the next morning if it hadn't been for James and Velmer and the guys.

"When're you going over to see the missionary?" they would ask each other.

"You're worse than I am. You ought to go."

"My big brother says he's going to take her into the bush, and when he brings her back, she'll forget all about being a sweet little missionary. She'll prob'ly like it so well she'll move right in with him."

Marvin laughed at that because he was afraid not to, but he

didn't think it was funny. Miss Emily wasn't that kind of a person and Ed Morin knew it. Besides he just talked big. He couldn't get *any* girl to go into the bush with him.

As the weeks passed, however, Marvin had other things to think about, although Aldina saw him several times and asked him to come to the meetings. His mother wrote again and she tried to sound cheerful. She asked what he was doing and how Jeremiah was getting along, but there was no deceiving him now. She wasn't getting any better.

He stuffed the letter into his shirt pocket and went to the store where he waited for his uncle's friend to finish with a customer. He had to talk to Laraviere about the letter. He didn't understand many of the words she used. And he wanted to ask Laraviere whether he thought it would do any good to see the missionary woman like Aldina had said. He couldn't see how this praying would help, but Laraviere would know about that. The white man ought to know if it was anything that would help his mother.

The Bay manager was holding a pair of moccasins between expert fingers when the boy approached him, determining the quality of the hide, the tanning, and the way they were sewed.

"It's good moose hide," the dark-skinned Cree said, squirming before him. It was not easy for an older woman to talk with a white man, even one like Laraviere, who was a friend to her people. "I tanned it myself."

"Ehe," Laraviere said. "The hide is good and the work is good, but you've got a family. Won't you need the moccasins this winter?"

She paused. *"Ehe."* Her voice was so low that Laraviere had to lean forward to catch what she was saying. "But they are hungry and the welfare check is gone."

"I couldn't give you more than two dollars a pair for them. That's the going price."

Her eyes gleamed. "I'll take it."

"And I'll have to charge you four dollars for them when I sell them back to you in November."

"Ehe."

"It isn't good to do that, Mrs. Burwyn. It costs you money that you need for your family."

"They have to have macaroni and lard and tea now," she said simply. She didn't say it, but Laraviere knew her reasoning. There was no point in worrying about what she would have to do when winter came. The problems that faced her now were so staggering that she had to concern herself with them and let the winter take care of itself.

Laraviere sighed. If her credit had been good, he would have been able to charge the supplies to her and let her pay for them when she had the money, but her credit had been shut off for a month and a half. He knew her problem. Her husband drank up everything he could put his hand on, so she had to order C.O.D.'s from Simpson-Sears and Eatons whenever she had a little money.

When Mrs. Burwyn left the store clutching her small sack of groceries and grumbling to herself, Laraviere turned back to Marvin.

"I didn't want to do it," he explained, as though the boy was questioning his motives. "But what could I do? Her credit's not worth a cent, and I couldn't afford to give her the grub she had to have." His breath was coming in quick, shallow stabs. "I won't get back half of what I've got out now." He found a chair and ponderously lowered himself into it. "I suppose I could've held the moccasins for security and loaned her the stuff, but the supervisor wouldn't have liked that. And besides, I got to look out for the company. They're the ones who pay my wages."

Marvin didn't understand what Laraviere was saying, but he nodded in agreement.

"Whatever you do, boy, don't ever get yourself boxed in that way. It's hard enough to make your money go 'round without throwing it away the way most everyone on the reserve does."

But Marvin was not listening. He tugged the envelope from his pocket and held it out.

"I got this from my mother today."

"*Ehe,*" the Frenchman said in flawless Cree. "I saw it when I sorted the mail."

"I don't like what it says."

Laraviere's thin smile was humorless. "I can't do much about that."

"I want you to read it and see if — if — " He wanted to know if her illness sounded as bad to Laraviere as it did to him, but he could not find words to voice the question. It was as though speaking of it would make it worse.

Laraviere read the short letter hurriedly, his beady little eyes sweeping the page.

"What do you think?" Marvin asked him.

Laraviere folded the letter with care. It would have been so easy to lie to the tense young boy who was pleading in such quiet desperation for news that his mother was going to get well.

But that wasn't the message from the boy's mother. Betty was trying to explain her illness. She wanted to tell him that she knew she would never see him again unless, miraculously, the dreaded operation brought a transformation to her body. And that wasn't likely, even with the new surgical techniques and drugs.

"What do you think?" the boy repeated.

"She's awful sick, Marvin. She's going to be in the hospital for a long time."

"And then?"

The Frenchman pulled himself erect as though to put an end to the conversation. But Marvin was not to be pushed aside.

"What about going to Miss Bannister?" the boy wanted to know.

Disapproval flecked Laraviere's narrowing eyes. "What for?"

"Somebody said she — she would pray for mom."

The Bay manager snorted.

"Wouldn't that do any good?"

"Not so's you could notice! You better leave your mother to the doctors. They're the only ones who can do anything for her now."

"Somebody told me Miss Bannister would pray for her," Marvin repeated, still studying the man's face.

"Sure!" The old Frenchman was bitter. "She'll pray for your mother! And she'll make you think she's gonna get well. But the truth is, Miss Bannister or no one else can do anything for her. If she's gonna die, even the doctors can't help her."

7

Marvin knew, even as he left the store and stumbled up the path towards his grandfather's cabin, that he was going to go and see the missionary lady. What else could he do? His mother was so sick that there was nothing anyone could do for her. Maybe Miss Bannister couldn't help either, but it couldn't do any harm to try.

He had already decided that he was going to visit the missionary, but he didn't think he would talk to her about his mother at first. He wanted to find out what her religion was like; he didn't understand anything about this praying business.

The next afternoon he was at Miss Bannister's house a few minutes before the meeting started. Most of the kids were already there. The girls sat on the chairs, two or three to each, while the boys sat on the floor or stood, self-consciously, near the door.

Aldina looked up and waved to him, and half the kids in the room saw it. He would have whirled and bolted from the room had it not been for his mother being so sick and the possibility, however faint, that Miss Bannister could help her. The smiling, freckled missionary signaled for them to be quiet.

"We're going to sing some songs this afternoon, but before we do, how many of you brought someone else to the meeting this afternoon."

Aldina's hand went up almost defiantly. "I did."

"And who did you bring?" Miss Bannister was searching the

faces of the girls for the faint smile that would indicate the one she had induced to come.

"I brought Marvin."

The kids snickered, and Marvin could have died. What was the matter with that stupid girl anyway? he reasoned angrily. Did she have to blab everything?

But Miss Bannister's eyes lighted and her smile warmed him in spite of his annoyance.

"That's nice. We're so glad you came, Marvin. We hope you come back again and bring a friend."

He muttered something, but afterwards he had no idea what he had said.

They sang a couple of songs and Miss Bannister did what she called praying. She had them all bow their heads and close their eyes while she talked out loud.

If that was what praying was, Marvin decided even before she got done, Laraviere was right. It sure wasn't anything that would help his mother.

He wanted to leave right then, but he couldn't do that. He liked Miss Bannister, and if he went out before she finished, it would only make her feel bad. So he listened as she told a story, placing pictures on a funny, cloth-covered board as she did so.

"There was a little short man who lived in the city of Jericho," she began. "He wasn't a good man. He had taken money that didn't belong to him, and very few people liked him. But he had heard that Jesus was coming to Jericho, and he wanted to see Him so much that he climbed a tree to look at Him. . . ."

When she had finished, the girls pleaded so loudly for another story that Miss Bannister told them about a blind man.

". . . And Jesus fixed his eyes so he wasn't blind any more."

Marvin thought about that. This praying business didn't sound like anything much to him, but if the guy called Jesus could make a blind man see, He just might be able to help his mother. If this Jesus would only come to the reserve, He could heal her lungs.

When the meeting was over, Marvin left with the other kids because he didn't know what else to do. He really wanted to stay around and see if Miss Bannister would tell him where this Jesus lived. If it wasn't too far away, maybe he could go and get Him to come.

That night sleep was slow in coming for Marvin, all he could think about was Jesus who had such a kind face. Jesus was going to make his mother well again. He knew it! All he had to do was go and talk to Miss Bannister! Then he was so excited that he didn't want to sleep, but lay there wishing the night away.

As soon as he had finished breakfast the following morning, Marvin rushed over to the cabin which the young missionary had rented. He knocked loudly on the door, but there was no answer.

He left the house and hurried to the store, thinking she might be there.

"What you want to see her for?" Laraviere demanded suspiciously.

Marvin was defensive. "I just want to talk to her for a couple of minutes, that's all."

"I heard you went over to her meeting yesterday." The white man's voice was harsh.

"I — I just wanted to find out what it was like."

"I told you already you should leave her alone! That guff'll only cause trouble for you, Marvin. It isn't for you."

"I — I just wanted to see her about something, that's all." He backed away.

"Don't you go near that woman again! You do and I'll tell Jeremiah on you, that's what I'll do!"

But by this time Marvin didn't care what Laraviere or anyone else said. He had to talk to the missionary lady. He didn't care who found out!

It was late afternoon when Emily Bannister finally came along the path towards her cabin. Marvin glanced over his shoulder to see if anyone was watching him and sped after her.

"Miss Emily!" he exclaimed, catching up with her. "Miss Emily?"

"*Ehe?*"

"I wondered if I could talk to you."

"Of course, Marvin." She stopped and faced him. "What is it?"

His gaze swept the area around them cautiously. "Not out here. Inside."

He followed her into the cabin and waited while she closed the door and asked him to sit down.

"Now what is it you wanted to talk to me about?"

"I've been thinking about this Jesus you've been talking about," he said.

"I'm glad to hear that, Marvin."

"I've got to go and see Him." Hurriedly he blurted out the story.

Marvin didn't understand what she tried to tell him then. She said something about Jesus dying and coming back to life again and being in heaven now.

She didn't say where heaven was, and he was afraid to ask her. It sounded too far away for him to go there, anyway.

Miss Emily must have known what he was thinking because she told him that they couldn't go to see Jesus until they died. But that wouldn't do his mother any good. She was awful sick. If he had to wait until he died to see Jesus, it wouldn't be in time to help her.

"But we can pray to Him, if you like, and ask Him to help your mother to get well so she can come back to the reserve."

Disgust gleamed in his narrowing eyes. "A lot of good that'll do!" He left without giving her a chance to say anything more.

When he got back to his grandfather's cabin, he wished he had never gone to hear the missionary. Laraviere had told, and the old man pounced on him fiercely.

"How many times do I have to tell you that the white man's ways are for the white man?"

Marvin did not reply.

"That woman's religion is not for you! You are Cree!" Jeremiah's eyes flashed.

"I just went to see her," Marvin retorted, his own temper rising. "That doesn't mean I'm going to follow her religion."

"You don't go over to her place any more. Do you hear?"

The boy stalked away, cheeks flaming. He hadn't planned on going back to see Miss Bannister any more, but still he didn't like the way his grandfather had talked to him. It made him want to go again to the missionary's meetings just to show him he could do as he pleased.

Only he didn't. There was no use in his going there any more. She couldn't help his mother.

Before the summer was over, Marvin got another letter from his mother. The handwriting was even shakier than before.

"I don't feel very good," she wrote. "I wish I weren't so far away so you could come and see me. I get so lonesome for you. . . . I hope you're being a good boy and minding your grandfather."

Towards the end of the letter she mentioned the operation again.

"The doctors still seem to think that I'll have to have it. They wanted to do it last week, but I caught cold, so they have to wait until I'm over my cold."

Jeremiah almost snatched the letter away from him. "Let me have that. I'm going to take it down to the store and have Laraviere read it to me."

"It's *my* letter!" Marvin snapped.

"I want to talk to Laraviere about it!"

Marvin knew better than to ask to go along.

The old man had Laraviere read the letter to him slowly three or four times; he studied out each sentence, each burning word.

"What do you think?" he asked when the Frenchman had finished.

"It is bad, Jeremiah." A haunting sadness tinged the store-keeper's voice. "Betty is awful sick. She may not get well."

Rabbit Ear wouldn't listen to that. Betty was his only daughter —his only child. She *had* to live! Didn't Laraviere understand that?

As quickly as his anger came, it subsided. He should know better than that. There was sorrow in Laraviere's voice as he explained about the letter. The Frenchman couldn't help it that the sickness of the lungs had taken hold of Betty and would not let go.

One final letter came from Marvin's mother — this time written to Jeremiah. The tests had been completed, she wrote, and the operation was to be the following day.

"They say that I'm not as strong as they would like to have me, but don't feel it wise to wait any longer."

Jeremiah thought about burning sweet grass and tobacco that night in an effort to get his spirit-helper to intervene, but he had no strength. And what good would it do? Hadn't Thunder spoken of the future?

A week later the Mounties came in by boat from Deauval. Jeremiah and Marvin were among those who went down to the dock to learn the purpose of the visit.

"I'm looking for Jeremiah Rabbit Ear," the young officer said.

Heads turned in Jeremiah's direction, and the people moved aside so the officer could approach the old man.

"I'm afraid I have bad news for you." He thrust a radiogram into Jeremiah's hands.

"W-what does it say?" he stammered.

The officer's eyes narrowed. "Oh- - -oh, I see." He opened the message and looked at it as though he didn't already know the contents. "Your daughter, Betty, died two days ago at the sanatorium in Saskatoon following an operation."

Jeremiah's expression did not change. Marvin, who was standing beside him, grasped the twisted fingers with his firm young hand. The old man looked down into the boy's face and then the two turned and started slowly up the long, narrow path towards their cabin. James Rediron approached Marvin hesitantly before they had gone a dozen steps.

"Here, I got this for you." He thrust a grubby piece of candy into Marvin's hand.

Marvin accepted it wordlessly. He knew it was James' way of expressing sympathy.

He and his grandfather were almost at the cabin when Marvin saw Aldina standing near an abandoned dog sled. She did not speak or wave, but tears flooded her dark eyes and she turned away quickly.

No one saw Marvin cry, even at his mother's funeral, but in the dead of night when the village was sleeping and the darkness hid his secret, he let the tears flow until his pillow was wet. He tried to remember his mother's smile, the way her eyes flashed when she was happy, and the hushed music of her voice. He tried to forget the ugly memories of the wine, the men, and the arguments.

8

Autumn wore a circlet of frost in her gold and vermillion hair. The shallow ponds were skimmed with ice every morning, and the leaves were beginning to drift down over the mulch of other years. The wind was losing its playful summer mood, and when it ripped out of the north, it locked the fishermen's boats on shore with savage, foam-etched breakers and the chill of winter that was soon to come.

Bruce Norris of the Department of Indian Affairs slouched behind the desk in the drafty Birch Lake schoolroom which he had appropriated as an office for a few days. He cursed the weather, his lack of foresight in taking such a job when he had graduated from college at midterm the year before, and he cursed the helpless people who had forced him out of his pleasant office in Prince Albert and brought him here.

Every fall a department representative had to travel to the reserves. There were loans to make for new traps, ammunition to distribute and a thousand nagging details to handle. And the people never seemed to learn, he reasoned. Every year the same men came shuffling in with the same questions, the same needs.

"There are times when I wonder why I ever went into the Indian Service," he had complained to his wife, Tina, the night before he was to go north. "They've got to be taken care of like so many babies. They can't even fill out a few forms and send them in. Someone from our office has to go out to the reserves and do it for them. And time doesn't mean a thing to them. It takes a week to get a day's work done out in the field."

She murmured her agreement.

"I know what I'd do if it were up to me. I'd make them stand on their own feet. Let them go hungry once in awhile and they'd soon learn to take care of themselves. It's ridiculous to have to change their diapers and burp them the way we do."

And the more Bruce Norris thought about it, sitting in the crude little schoolroom, the angrier he became. He took out his pipe, tamped a double pinch of tobacco into it, and struck a match. They'd better not come in wanting any special favors. There was only one way to treat these people. Be tough enough with them to make them accept a little responsibility for themselves.

The door opened and an elderly Cree shuffled hesitantly inside. "*Waaci.*"

"Speak English, man! What do you want?"

The old man stared at him blankly.

"What is it? What do you want?"

The Indian only knew a few words of English. He couldn't understand the angry young man.

"Go over there and sit down."

The man did not move.

"Go and sit down." Norris motioned jerkily towards a chair along the wall.

Mutely the graying Cree shuffled over to the chair and lowered himself into it.

Bruce was still fuming. He supposed he should get an interpreter to find out what the old man wanted, but when he had arrived by plane the day before, the interpreter they usually used was out in the bush checking his trap line. Well, let the old man sit there. He didn't have anything else to do. Bruce busied himself at his desk, ignoring the perplexed Indian who was waiting for him.

The following afternoon Marvin went into the Hudson Bay Store with a list of things his grandfather wanted. Laraviere puffed his way from one shelf to the other putting the order together.

62

"You're going to have quite a load, Marvin. Sure you can lug all of it up the hill?"

"*Ehe.*"

"If you want to leave part of it, I'll bring it up when I close the store. I wouldn't mind seeing Jeremiah, anyway."

"I can manage."

"Suit yourself."

"Oh, I almost forgot. He wants a box of .22 long rifles."

Laraviere stopped what he was doing and slowly turned to focus his gaze on the boy.

"You sure those are for your grandfather, Marvin?"

"*Ehe.*"

"He ain't fixin' to use no .22 shells to go out after moose is he?"

Marvin shrugged. "He didn't say what he wants 'em for."

"If he keeps fooling around with that .22 of his, he's gonna get himself killed. Doesn't he know Indian Affairs has a man here now? He can get shells free for his big rifle"

"Yesterday he went over to get some like he did last year, but he didn't get any."

"How come?"

Marvin shrugged his shoulders.

"All he told me was that I should get a box of .22 long rifles and put 'em on his bill."

The Hudson Bay manager stuffed the box of shells in his pocket.

"I'll go over and see Jeremiah. I'll take 'em to him."

This seemed strange to Marvin, but he didn't question Laraviere.

At 4:30 Laraviere closed the store and walked across to the schoolhouse to see Bruce Norris. The Indian Affairs representative would be eating dinner with him in an hour, but the Frenchman couldn't wait that long.

Bruce smiled broadly when he saw Laraviere. "You don't know how good it is to see a white face after what I've been looking at all day."

The Frenchman's eyes were cold and hostile. "They tell me that Jeremiah Rabbit Ear was in here to get some rifle shells."

The young man frowned. "Rabbit Ear? Rabbit Ear? I don't remember anyone by that name." He began to scan his list. "Nope. His name isn't here."

"Kind of an old man," Laraviere persisted. "A little stiff with arthritis."

Bruce scratched his ear. "Oh, yes, I remember him." He started to laugh. "Sat around here for awhile yesterday."

"He sat here *all day* yesterday!" the Bay manager informed him icily.

"I guess that's right, now that I think of it. I couldn't get around to him. The old guy can't speak English. I didn't know what he wanted."

"You could've found out. That's what you come out here for."

Bruce's laughter had a hollow, defensive ring.

"Don't get so upset about such a little thing as that. He didn't have anything else to do. He might as well be sitting here as out on the dock or over in your store pestering you."

The flames leaped high in the big Frenchman's eyes. "Jeremiah's entitled to that ammo, Norris. You don't have no right to treat him the way you did."

"Well, don't have a stroke over it. He doesn't need to be in such a hurry to get a moose. He can eat macaroni for a couple more days."

Laraviere jerked the .22 long rifles from his pocket and slammed them resoundingly on the desk in front of Norris.

"These're what he sent his grandson to get for him because he don't have the money to buy cartridges for that big rifle of his. Do you want to get him killed going after a moose with a .22?"

"That's his lookout — not mine." Norris shrugged, and his lips curled bitterly about the words. "Tell him to come in and I'll give him his cartridges. You and I don't have to fight about them."

"I'll get them for him myself!" Laraviere strode around the desk, picked up a box of high-powered shells and emptied half of them into his hand. "Jeremiah's already been here to see you. I ain't having him treated that way again — by you or anyone else!"

"You get out of those!" Bruce sprang to intercept him. "I'll take care of it!"

"You had your chance. Now take your arm off me!"

Norris stepped back.

"Those cartridges are government property. I could send the RCMP in after you for taking them!"

"You just do that, sonny boy!" The Bay manager pushed close to him, his temper exploding. "You just have the RCMP come in after me! I'd like that!"

Flushing, Norris retreated to his desk.

Word of the argument between Laraviere and Norris blanketed the reserve before the sun went down. Men told each other about it, eyes sparkling, and the women related the account as they tended fires under the fish they were smoking. James Rediron asked Marvin about it the next morning.

"All I know is that he brought some cartridges over to the house last night and told grandfather that they were for him to use when he goes after moose."

The other boy's grin was wide. "I'd like to've been there and heard it! They say Norris was so mad he wanted to fight Laraviere."

Marvin nodded. He had heard that, too, only it wouldn't have been much of a fight. The Frenchman was so big that the only thing the Indian Affairs guy would have had to fear was being stepped on.

The boys walked down to the lake shore together.

"When I get big," James boasted, finding strength in the Hudson Bay manager's act, "I'm not takin' anything off of anybody. And if the Indian Agent gets in my way, it's gonna be too bad for him! I'll tell him off, too!"

"Hmmmm," Marvin murmured.

"They say Laraviere told this new guy he had to get off the reserve today."

"I heard that George Beardy told him to leave."

"Beardy! He's like your grandfather! He's scared to say anything to Indian Affairs!"

"He is not!"

"Ask any of the guys. They'll tell you!"

Marvin knew what he meant. When the older guys gathered at one cabin or the other to drink beer, gamble, and talk about their girls, they often muttered darkly of what they would do if they were *okimaaw*. And they always ended the conversation by finding fault with everything George Beardy did or didn't do.

Usually it bothered Marvin to hear such talk about his grandfather's friend. But not today. Thinking about what Laraviere had done gave him a warm feeling of power that he had never known. In a way he felt much the same as James did, only he couldn't imagine himself standing up to a man like the Indian Agent. Of course, he couldn't imagine James doing it either.

9

After his mother died, the months plodded by with leaded feet. As winter died to give birth to spring, Marvin began to forget the memories that hurt so much. All he recalled were the good things that could gladden his heart.

His grandfather found new strength after his daughter's death. Marvin wasn't sure, but he thought it had something to do with the Thunder's promise that he would live long enough to see his grandson become a man.

Even as Jeremiah seemed to draw new strength from some hidden resource, he became more dependent on his spirit-helper. He called on the Thunder for everything and was more insistent than ever that Marvin, too, worship the spirits.

"A long time ago," he would begin, "when our people were fighting the white man, a brave and two friends were trapped by some soldiers. The brave's helper was the Stone-spirit.

" 'Quick!' his spirit told him. 'Get off your horse and hunch over on your knees and elbows!'

"He did as he was told and tried to get his friends to do the same, but they were too afraid. His spirit-helper changed him into a stone until the soldiers were gone, but his friends were killed."

Marvin didn't believe stories like that, but he wasn't going to say anything that would let his grandfather know that he scorned his beliefs. There was no use in breaking the heart of the only one he had left in the world.

"You should have a spirit-helper," his grandfather concluded.

Marvin did not answer him. Why should he bother with the spirits? They couldn't help his mother. Why should he believe they could do anything to help him? He was going to take care of himself.

As Aldina grew older and her figure began to develop into womanhood, she looked at the boys in the village with increased interest, but she also found time to visit Miss Emily Bannister. She had a feeling that her mother didn't like it, and Aldina suspected that she would dislike it a great deal more if her daughter got interested in this God Miss Emily kept talking about.

Her suspicion was confirmed when she talked with her mother about Rose Starkey, a friend her own age, who also was often at the missionary's little cabin.

"Why does she go there?" Mary demanded.

Aldina pretended not to know.

"Her mother says she is over at the missionary's house more than she's home. What does she do?"

The girl saw that she had to answer her. "They sew sometimes," she said reluctantly, "and play crokinole or checkers."

But her mother wasn't interested in the games. "What else does she do?"

"How should I know?" Aldina hitched her shoulders forward expressively. "She talks, I guess."

"About God?"

"Sometimes."

Mary left what she was doing and came over to stand before her daughter. "The women are saying that Rose says she is walking the way of this white woman's God?"

"—I guess so." She studied her mother curiously, waiting for the storm that was certain to break.

Fury darkened Mary's face and narrowed her eyes, intensifying her hostility. "Her mother should beat her until she changes her mind!"

"But Miss Emily says it is the only way to get to heaven!" Aldina hadn't intended to say that; the words had escaped in an unguarded instant.

68

Mary Brouilette turned back to the stove quickly, stunned by the revelation that her own daughter was being influenced by the red-haired missionary. She took the long fork with trembling fingers and stabbed a piece of meat in the stew. But before she checked to see that it was done, she pivoted once more to face Aldina.

"You don't walk the Jesus way, do you?" she demanded, concern in her voice.

Rebellion seethed behind sullen eyes. She didn't walk the Jesus way, but what if she wanted to? She wouldn't ask her mother or anyone else if she could. She was going to run her own life.

"Do you?" Mary was close to tears.

"No, I don't, but I just might some time!"

"I want you to be a good girl, Aldina," Mary muttered, "but I want you to have fun, too. If you walk the Jesus way, you won't ever be able to do nothing."

The remark disturbed Aldina, and she thought about it often. Miss Emily hadn't told them anything like that when she told the stories and made the pictures on the cloth-covered board.

She didn't know how her mother could have known such a thing about being a Christian when she claimed not to know anything about Miss Emily's God. But Aldina didn't want to ask Miss Emily about it.

She soon decided that her mother must have been right about Christians not being able to do much of anything. Rose hadn't been a believer, as Miss Emily called it, more than a month, and already there were things she wouldn't do.

She didn't tell stories like the rest of the girls did, or swear, or pick up candy or a pretty scarf in the store when Laraviere wasn't watching. Aldina knew those weren't the sort of things her mother was talking about when she said a Christian couldn't do anything, for her parents would have beaten her if they ever caught her stealing. But walking the Jesus way had changed Rose, and Aldina wasn't sure that she liked the change. Finally she quit going to the missionary's house.

Late that summer when the wife of one of the government officials accompanied her husband to the reserve, she stopped to visit Mary Brouilette. The woman had taken a liking to Aldina ever since the beautiful, sharp-eyed little vixen was big enough to climb up on her knee. She knew Aldina had always done well in school and felt that the girl had the capability to go through high school and perhaps on to college.

"It would be nice if Aldina could go out to school next year, Mary," she suggested.

Mary Brouilette squinted her disapproval. That would take her youngest daughter away from home, and she would be gone for months.

"I wouldn't like to have her gone," she said honestly.

"I'm sure I would feel the same way," the white woman acknowledged, "but Aldina is a daughter who could make you very proud of her."

Mary looked out the window in time to see Aldina go into Miss Emily's cabin on one of her infrequent visits. If Aldina went away to school, she would be away from home, but she would also be away from the influence of the missionary.

"Do you think she could get in school somewhere?" she asked numbly.

"There's no question about it. I'll see to it myself, if it's all right with you."

"We'll ask her."

So Aldina went to a boarding school in the southern part of the province. She liked going to a school where there were plenty of classrooms, new books, and where the teacher had time to help her if she had difficulty with a lesson, which wasn't often.

Aldina liked living in the dorm with the other girls her own age. She liked being away from home. There was always something to do if she slipped away from the dorm and their trusting, easy-to-deceive housemother. It was simple to get past her and back in again, so simple that there were times when it irritated Aldina.

When Aldina was fourteen, she had her first date. He was all right, she guessed, but he sure wasn't much fun. She wasn't going to date any guys her own age again, she promised herself.

70

She was going with one of the juniors or seniors like Raymond Sample. She told some of the girls she was going to get him to ask her for a date, and they laughed at her.

"You don't even know him."

"It that so?"

"My brother's a good friend of his, and they both think girls our age are a drag."

"You wait. You just wait."

Aldina really didn't know Raymond Sample, but that wasn't going to stop her. Before the week was out, she had contrived to stand next to him in the cafeteria line.

"How come I haven't met you before?" he asked.

Aldina shrugged. "You don't like girls my age."

"Who said that?"

"Isn't it true?"

"I'd be out of my mind if I said that."

They went to a table and sat across from each other. Before they finished eating, he had asked her for a date for that night.

The following week the school police officer caught Aldina and Raymond in the back seat of one of the faculty cars.

"You get your clothes on, both of you!" the Indian officer stormed.

"What are you going to do to us?" she asked tearfully.

"Get dressed and you'll find out!"

She pleaded with him, but soon learned that was useless. They were both hauled before the superintendent and dismissed from school, but not before there was a lot of talk about taking Aldina to a doctor to see whether or not she was pregnant.

She cried again when they told her she would be sent home.

"I'll just die," she moaned.

Aldina would probably have gone back to the reserve without protest had she been able to get a plane north immediately, but there was no space for her the first two days, and on the morning of the third day a front moved in that kept all aircraft grounded for a week. By the time they were flying once more, she had made friends with a couple of men on a lumbering crew and had slipped away with them into the bush.

10

MARVIN, A SPIDERY, lean-faced fifteen-year-old, hitched forward in the chair across from the Hudson Bay manager, his nervous gaze jerking restlessly about the sparsely furnished store office. Although the manager was his friend, he could not bring himself to look directly at him.

"How old are you now?" Laraviere asked.

Marvin licked his lips. "Fifteen."

"I was talking to your grandfather the other day. I'd like to see you go off to school and make something of yourself."

Marvin did not answer him. He and his grandfather had talked often about his going away to school.

"I don't like it," Jeremiah had said. "That Brouilette girl went, and where is she now?"

"Hmmmm," Marvin murmured. Going away to school would relieve some of the deadly boredom that was gripping him as he grew older. Still, he didn't know how he would like going to a strange place and living with people he didn't know.

"What do you think, Marvin? Interested?" Laraviere questioned.

Marvin tugged at the collar of his faded wool shirt.

"You don't want to stick around here where there isn't any work. You'll get to gambling and drinking and won't amount to anything. You don't want to be caught in the trap that gets so many of the young guys like you."

"Hmmmm."

72

"I'll tell you what I'll do. You go out to high school, and when you're done, I'll pay your way through college. Okay?"

Marvin wasn't sure that interested him at all. "Grandfather thinks I'd better stay here. He says he can teach me what I need to know."

"*Ehe.*" Laraviere leaned back and folded his hands across his broad stomach. He knew when he was defeated. Marvin was quoting his grandfather but expressing his own opinion. Further pressure would only forge a barrier between them. "If you ever change your mind, let me know. The offer holds."

Marvin was relieved. That was one of the things he liked about the Frenchman. He didn't try to push a guy into something he didn't want to do. At least he didn't shove too hard.

"If you won't go to school, I've been thinking about something else. How'd you like to come in the store and help me?"

Marvin stared at him. Laraviere actually meant it! He wanted him to work in the store.

"You'd have to be able to write down the orders. You can read and write good, can't you?"

The boy hesitated at the question. The old Frenchman knew as well as he that he could read and write. He had insisted on seeing every report card he ever brought home. If his marks were good, he had given him a couple of candies. If they were bad, he had scolded him severely.

"I've been to school," he replied.

Laraviere nodded, forming a tipi with his hands. "I wish you'd go on to school, but I think you'll do for a clerk. I think you'll do just fine."

So Marvin went to work at the store, waiting on customers and writing down their orders when they charged. His friends came in to try him as soon as he started work. They showed up at noon while Laraviere was home for dinner.

"How about a couple of packs of cigarettes?" James asked, grinning.

"You got the money?"

"Money!" He acted surprised. "We're friends, ain't we?"

"Yeh," Velmer put in. "You wouldn't expect us to pay for a couple of packs of cigarettes, would you?"

"Give me the money first. Then you'll get your cigarettes."

"Old Frenchie'll never miss 'em." Velmer's laugh filled the store. "Besides, the Bay's got lots of cigarettes."

Marvin was immovable. "Not to give away, they ain't."

While Velmer talked to him, James had slipped around the counter and opened the glass, taking out a box of tobacco.

"Get out of there!" Marvin sprang towards him.

"I just took one tin." James backed away. "That won't hurt nothin'. Old Frenchie'd prob'ly give it to me if he was here."

"He never gave you any tobacco in his life." Marvin pushed close to him and James backed away. "I want that tobacco, Red-iron."

"Aw c'mon," Velmer said. "What's one little tin of tobacco?"

Marvin backed James against the wall. "I don't want to have to ask you again."

Rediron's face flushed darkly, but he still managed an air of bravado. "S'pose I tell you that you've got to take it away from me if you want it?"

"I can do that, too." With one hand Marvin grasped James by the collar and hauled him close; with the other he wrenched the tobacco tin free.

"A fine friend you are!"

"Just don't try anything like that again!"

Laraviere came in as the two boys slunk out. "What's going on?" he demanded.

"Nothing."

"Have any trouble?"

Marvin busied himself at the shelves. "Not exactly. We just had a few words."

The Bay manager said no more. He had been expecting something like this. And from the looks on the faces of James and Velmer, Marvin had passed the test.

The only part of the job that Marvin disliked was having to tell those who had charged their limit that they could buy nothing more on credit until they had made payments on their bill. The people didn't resent it; they were used to having that happen. He and his grandfather had faced it often. But he still didn't like to refuse them credit. It was against the way of the Cree to refuse someone in need.

On Saturday night Laraviere called him into the office and sat down to write out his first check. "You've done a good job. You're going to make a fine clerk for the Bay. Who knows? Maybe you'll get to be manager someday."

Marvin said nothing. His very first check! Pride surged within him.

The storekeeper paused and looked up. The boy saw his indecision and cringed inwardly.

"Is there something wrong?"

A crooked grin lifted one corner of Laraviere's thin lips. "What's your last name?"

"Rabbit Ear." Marvin spoke hesitantly, as though the stigma was increased by having to reveal his illegitimate origin. Even though he was talking to a friend who thought no less of him for it, he still felt the shame.

"Rabbit Ear?" The Frenchman's lips curled distastefully. "That name's all right for your grandfather, but what kind of a name is it for a guy your age?"

Marvin had no answer for him.

"How's it going to look on my records? 'Marvin Rabbit Ear works for Laraviere.' What're they going to think of that at the company office in Winnipeg? I'd be the laughingstock of the whole organization."

Marvin's nervousness rushed back. He didn't know why Laraviere had to make such a big deal of it. There wasn't anything he could do.

"Haven't you got any other name?"

He shook his head.

"You must have. What was your father's name?"

"My mother never told me." He spoke so low that the big Frenchman had trouble hearing him.

The Bay manager pushed the check book aside and got to his feet thoughtfully. "We've got to do something about this. We

75

can't have you going through life with a name like Rabbit Ear."
He leaned against the desk. "Your mother had a lot of 'friends,'
Marvin. Is there one that you liked better than the rest?"

"I didn't want any of them to come around."

Laraviere nodded. He could understand that. "But wasn't
there one of them that you liked just a little bit?"

"There was one who did treat me a little better than some of
the others," the boy said at last. "He didn't knock me around
much — only when he was drunk."

"Now we're gettin' some place. What was his name?"

Marvin had trouble remembering that, too. The guy had left
the reserve, and he hadn't seen him since before his mother died.
Finally he pulled the name out of the depths of the past.

"Harold was his first name," he exclaimed. "Harold Cinder!"

Laraviere stared at him. "You've got to be pulling my leg. Nobody's named Cinder."

"He was. His name was Harold Cinder."

Laraviere snorted. "Cinder! I'd as soon have you called Rabbit
Ear." He waddled back to his chair and lowered himself into it.
"Cinder. Cinder." He picked up a pencil and wrote the name.
"That's horrible."

Marvin squirmed. "Maybe we can think of another one," he
said lamely.

"No, there's got to be a way to make a decent name out of
Cinder." His round face lighted. "Why didn't I think of it before? We'll give you a proud name —a solid French name that
no one will snicker at. From now on you're Marvin Lacendre."

Marvin nodded. His last name meant little to him one way or
the other as long as it satisfied Laraviere. He took the newly
written check, noted the figures with pride, and stuffed it into his
pocket. No one else his age in the village had ever had a check of
their own before — one they had earned. It was a proud day for
him.

Jeremiah had not protested when Marvin told him that Laraviere had offered him a job in the store, but he was deeply disturbed.

"Working inside is all right for Laraviere," he confided in

George Beardy. He's a white man, and they've got strange ways, like selling things and buying furs. But it's not for Marvin."

"It is good to have a store on the reserve," the chief reminded him.

"*Ehe,* it is good to have a store on the reserve so a man's wife and little ones don't have to go hungry when his luck is bad and he can't get a moose. And it is good to have a place where we can sell our furs."

"*Ehe,*" Beardy broke in. "It helps all of us to have someone like Laraviere to buy our skins. We can trust him. The prices he gives are fair."

"But," Jeremiah continued firmly, "working in such a place, even with a man like Laraviere, is not for the Cree. Hunting and trapping and fishing are the proper jobs for our people. The great spirit *Manitow* has so ordered our affairs."

Beardy had to agree with him. An Indian shouldn't be tied to the inside of a building selling candies to children or macaroni and flour to their mothers. It was better for him to be on the trap line.

There was another reason Jeremiah had, however, for wanting his grandson out of the store and off in the bush. If Marvin were away from the settlement, he would not be so tempted by the enticing smiles of the wrong kind of girls: girls who had been lured into the bush almost from the time they quit playing with dolls and who soon learned there was one way to get practically anything they wanted from men and boys. And on the trail Marvin would be away from the destructive power of the cheap wine that had been such a curse to his mother. So, Jeremiah had not been thinking only of himself when he tried to persuade Marvin to come back to the old ways of their people. He was thinking of the boy and the bad things that could happen to him. But Marvin was not ready to listen. He enjoyed having something to do and getting a check every Saturday night. He enjoyed having the guys seek him out, too, and being invited to their parties.

"Come on over to Vetel's tonight," one or the other would say softly. "A few of the guys're getting together."

77

As soon as he could get away from his grandfather after supper, Marvin would slip over to Vetel's where the drinking and the poker had already started.

"Here comes a guy with some money." They tried to joke, but envy crept into their voices. "Now the game'll be interesting."

"You don't expect me to put up real money against a lot of IOU's, do you?"

"Next week the welfare checks'll be in," James Rediron joked. "Then we'll all have a little money."

"Yeh, how about loanin' us a few bucks 'til we get our checks, okay?"

Marvin pretended not to hear them.

"At least you can buy a few bottles of wine," Velmer told him.

He usually wound up buying most of it. He complained once in a while, but he really didn't mind. It gave him a sense of importance to be able to furnish the liquor for everybody, even if it did make his weekly check disappear.

As the game wore on, James Rediron told of seeing Bruce Norris get off the Canso that afternoon.

"He had another guy with him."

"I think I'll go over and see him tomorrow," Velmer said.

"He won't give you no cartridges. Besides, you couldn't hit a moose if you did find one," James taunted.

"I don't want no cartridges. I figured I'd get a loan to buy traps and go out on the trap line this fall."

"You couldn't trap no beaver neither," Marvin added.

Velmer argued with him, but he was unconvinced. Marvin knew he was the only one of the guys who had ever spent a season on the trapline. But even he hadn't trapped alone.

"There's better money fishing," James put in, "and it's easier, too."

"I know, but I don't have any nets either."

Vetel sighed. "There ought to be some place where a guy could get a job here on the reserve." He looked up at Marvin. "Why don't you quit what you're doin' so I can go to work at the store?" He was joking, of course, but envy crept into his voice.

"You couldn't work in a store," Rediron scoffed. "You'd have to be able to read and write to hold a job with the Bay."

"If Marvin can do it, I can, too." The wine was beginning to work on his tongue.

Marvin Lacendre reached for the bottle. "Why don't you guys shut up and have some more wine?"

The next afternoon the young man who had come in with Norris sauntered into the Hudson Bay store and bought a coke.

"This is my first visit to the north," he told Marvin. "I figured I'd better come up with Bruce while I had a chance to take him up on his invitation. Guess this is his last trip."

Marvin was curious about that, but he kept every trace of his personal interest in the Indian Affairs representative from his voice. "Is he getting another job?"

The other man shook his head. "Nope, he's goin' back to school, from what he says. He tells me he's seen so much sickness and misery in the north that he's decided he wants to go into medicine so he can help people." His cynicism was barbed. "But if you ask me, he's doin' it to make a buck. That's the reason most guys become doctors these days."

They were still talking when Bruce Norris came in looking for Laraviere.

"I'm back here," the Frenchman sang out. "Come on back!"

The government man found his way to the little office and took a chair across from the big roll-top desk. "I've been doing a lot of thinking about what happened between you and me the last time I was here," he began.

"Forget it," Laraviere broke in roughly. "It was just one of those things."

Marvin, who was standing a short distance away, was surprised by the conversation. The other white man said something to him, but he did not answer, so intent was he in hearing what Laraviere and his caller were talking about.

"It means a lot to me," Bruce continued. "I went to Jeremiah a little while ago. Now I want to ask your forgiveness. I'm sorry for the attitude I've had towards the people here and towards you. Will you forgive me?"

"What brings this on?" Laraviere asked.

Bruce laughed nervously. "I suppose this will sound weird to you, but I have decided to let Jesus Christ have first place in my life. I'm trying to get things straightened out on this trip, since I won't be back any more."

The old Frenchman snorted his derision. "If it makes you feel better, I guess it's all right." Scorn honed an edge to his voice. "You sound just like that woman missionary who's leavin' here next week." His laughter was mocking. "She's been here for years trying to convert the women and kids, but they've been too smart to fall for that stuff she puts out."

11

JEREMIAH RABBIT EAR was glad Miss Emily Bannister was gone and would no longer be talking with the women and children about this Jesus. He only hoped she did not come back. It was not good to have such words hammering on the ears of those weak enough to be swayed by them.

Still, he had to admit that something had happened to change the fellow from Indian Affairs. He thought often about Bruce Norris and his strange visit. Norris had claimed that Jesus Christ had changed his life and had replaced his hate for the Indian with love.

Jeremiah could not understand anything like that. But he had more pressing problems than the white man's religion. He had wanted to get Marvin out in the bush, but now that he worked in the store it was impossible. He was held to the village by his job and by his friends who were already following the path of drunkenness, gambling, and immorality.

There was no knowing how his grandson was with girls, although Jeremiah had seen them sidling up to him. He hoped Marvin wasn't letting them take tobacco and soft drinks without paying for them.

"That's not the way you taught me," he retorted proudly when his grandfather asked him about it.

"I didn't teach you to drink wine, either," the old man reminded him.

A quick flush spread across the boy's cheeks, and he stalked out of the cabin. When he came stumbling back, long after midnight, his steps were uncertain and the stench of wine was heavy on his breath.

It hurt Jeremiah to see his only grandson benumbed by liquor, but he did no more than talk with him, and that infrequently. A Cree might slap his children around if they irritated him, especially if he was drunk; but when it came to discipline, he punished them rarely or not at all. A child might get sick and die, and if that happened after he had been punished, the parents would feel terrible. And so the average young Cree reached adult life with a minimum of discipline.

On several occasions, however, Jeremiah tried to encourage Marvin to live differently than he had been living. Once he even dared to ask him to go out on the trap line again.

"It's going to be a good year for beaver. There is sign everywhere," he remarked as they sat at the supper table.

Marvin reached for another helping of the macaroni that so often replaced the smoked fish and pemmican since he had started working at the store.

A sigh stirred Jeremiah. "I think I make more on my traps than you do working in the Bay. If you'll help me this year, Marvin, we'll both do good."

His grandson acted as though he was about to leave, but the old man stopped him with a glance. "It isn't easy for me to make the sets and walk the trap line alone."

Marvin's cheeks darkened. His grandfather was waiting for an answer. "I can't go with you. I've got a job."

"A job?" The word was a curse on Jeremiah's lips. "White man's work!"

"I get paid good."

The old man's anger surged.

When Marvin was eighteen, Howard Sturgeon moved his family to Birch Lake from one of the southern reserves. A gaunt, hawk-faced man with his common-law wife and a beautiful daughter, Sturgeon soon sought out Jeremiah and told him that he, too, had a spirit-helper.

"I was the most powerful medicine man on our reserve," he boasted.

"He is not a strong medicine man," Jeremiah told Marvin that night after his first introduction to Sturgeon.

"He says he does big things."

Jeremiah grunted. "I know what he says. But a man with a strong spirit-helper who can do big things does them. He doesn't have to brag like a girl with her first baby."

While Howard Sturgeon was trying to impress Jeremiah, Beardy, and the other important men in the village, his daughter, Ella, was impressing the boys. She was quiet, but lights danced in her eyes and she was as graceful and as self-assured as a blue heron feeding in the rushes.

Her hair shone in the sunlight like the coat of *Mahkwa*, the bear, in the fall when his belly is full of berries and he is fat and sleek. Her lips were the color of wild roses, and all the boys and some of the men sought her favors, but her most tantalizing smile was saved for Marvin.

She was a girl who usually got what she wanted, and before the new moon came, she was occupying most of his nights when he wasn't working. Marvin was too shy to talk of marriage, but she understood that this was his intention.

But there were problems. "My father will not let anyone marry me who doesn't have a spirit-helper."

His eyes slitted. "Don't tell me you're a spirit worshiper?"

"Aren't you?"

"Me?" Marvin laughed.

Some men could go through the motions of calling on the spirits whether they believed in them or not. But Marvin was different. He had to think about the matter honestly, turning it over in his mind, weighing its strengths and weaknesses.

It was fall again, and the bite of the coming winter lay lightly on the breath of the wind. Snow fingered the beach and blanketed the clearings with a frosty sheen no thicker than the bark on a birch, and the bays were beginning to freeze. Already the float-planes had been hauled out of the water to be fitted with skis while waiting, immobilized for a few short weeks, by the changing seasons.

The pace on the reserve quickened. The women were busy making mittens and repairing snowshoes for the day when the soft drifts would swallow trails and streams. The men were getting out their traps and coming into the store to make arrangements for supplies, borrowing against the catch of furs they would be taking.

Marvin watched with growing restlessness. He liked the store and the work he had been doing. He liked the respect with which the people treated him and the thought that some day he might be the manager.

Still, he was not satisfied.

During the past few weeks the walls of the store had been closing in about him, squeezing his chest until he could not breathe. His grandfather had said the store was no place for a Cree, and lately he began to wonder if his grandfather might be right. Some mornings he even hated to go to work and dreaded having to talk with a customer.

He didn't have any traps of his own, but he could get a loan from Indian Affairs, or he could use the money Laraviere was keeping for him. But when he talked with the Frenchman about it, Laraviere was against it.

"You're no trapper, Marvin," he said bluntly. "You'd starve to death."

The boy did not answer him, for deep within he shared the Bay manager's doubts about his own ability to handle a trap line. The only trapping he had done was with his grandfather who picked out the locations and supervised the making of the sets. He could probably get Jeremiah to go with him again, but everybody in the village would know about it and laugh at him.

It was then that Marvin began to think seriously about getting a spirit-helper. He didn't know whether or not he believed in the spirit, but the way he looked at it, there couldn't be any harm in trying it for awhile. If it did work out, he might do better with his traps. If it didn't, he could forget the whole business.

Once inside the cabin, he padded silently over to the corner where his grandfather kept the tobacco and sweet grass. He took a pinch of each and lighted them on the tin lid of the airtight heater. In the darkness he could not see the smoke, but he could smell its heady aroma. His pulse quickened as he slipped out of his moccasins and pants and crawled into his bedroll on the floor.

Almost as soon as he closed his eyes, he fell asleep and began to dream. A gray horse appeared to him, a broad, stocky animal that looked to be well broken to harness.

"If you worship me," the gray horse began, "I will help you in the bush and on the lake. And if you have enemies, I will punish them."

For some reason Marvin didn't like the gray horse. He didn't sound as though he would be worth the trouble.

At the store the next morning Laraviere saw the concern in his young clerk's eyes and misread it. "You aren't thinking about going out on that trap line yet, are you?"

Marvin did not reply. If he did decide to leave, he wouldn't tell Laraviere. It would be easier not to show up for work some Monday morning. He could take his traps and his gear from the store on Saturday afternoon and be out on the trap line before the manager even knew he had gone.

"If you quit, I might not be able to take you back," Laraviere persisted.

"*Ehe*," Marvin replied, his voice devoid of expression.

That night Marvin swore Ella to secrecy and shared his thinking with her. Disbelief gleamed in her eyes.

"Are you out of your mind?"

"The price of fur is going to be good this season."

"But maybe you don't catch good. Then you won't have any money for wine."

"I'll catch good," he told her doggedly.

"But I won't see you for so long." Her disappointment was evident.

"You could go with me."

"All winter on a trap line?"

She thought about that. "It's so lonely out in the bush. I want to be where there's some excitement."

Marvin wasn't angry that Ella did not want to go with him.

Nor was he persuaded to stay at home and spend the winter working in the store. If she didn't want to go, he would go alone.

The following Saturday while Laraviere was in his office, Marvin took the traps and supplies he needed, making out a bill that listed each item and the price. He wrote a note telling the manager what he had done and where he was going. His grandfather, elated at his decision to leave the store, wanted to go out in the bush with him, but Marvin refused.

"I go alone."

"*Ehe*, I understand. But I've taught you well. You'll bring in plenty of beaver blankets and muskrats and mink."

Marvin wasn't so sure about that. He still didn't have a *Mistabeo* to help him, and he wasn't sure that he knew enough about trapping, but he had to find out.

Sunday morning he put his gear and traps on his sled and drove off with his dogs. Even though he was sure Laraviere was still in bed, he went the opposite direction from the Bay property. He made his way down the lake half a mile or so before going out on the ice and angling back to get to the trail on the opposite shore.

Marvin had never experienced the real loneliness of the trap line, the ache for the sound of another human voice. Before, he had been with his grandfather. There had been endless hours when they didn't talk at all, but they could have if they had wanted to, and that was the difference.

The first day he got the cabin in order, putting a piece of cardboard in a window where the glass had been broken and fixing the door so it would close tighter. In the evening when he was getting the flour for bannock out of his grub box, he found a strange envelope in it. He studied it curiously for a moment before he opened it.

Tobacco and sweet grass! He had forgotten he would need them if he was going to call a spirit to be his helper, but his grandfather had remembered.

"The old fox!" he said aloud. "The old fox!"

After supper Marvin burned a little sweet grass and tobacco to summon the spirits and crawled into his bedroll. As he slept an exquisitely beautiful Indian girl appeared to him. Her dress was of the whitest caribou hide, intricately beaded. The delicate hollow of her throat was half covered with necklaces of beads and shining stones. She must have liked jewelry, for there were bracelets on both arms and rings on every finger. A sparkling tiara accentuated the gleaming blackness of her hair, which was braided and hung almost to her waist. Lights danced in her eyes like the sun in two glimmering pools, and her smile was as warm and inviting as a spring breeze.

"I would like to be your spirit," she said quietly.

Marvin liked that. The gray horse had been as brazen as a white woman. This one was reserved and shy, a proper Cree girl.

"If you worship me — if you bring me cloth and beads and bracelets — I will help you with money and bring good luck to your hunting and your traps."

"What about the fishing?" he asked. "Can you help me with that?" He might just as well be honest with her. If she didn't think she could help him in the ways he wanted help, he'd look for another spirit.

"*Ehe.* I can fill your nets with whites and yellows."

That was good, he thought, if she could really do it.

"And I can bring you a girl as beautiful as I am," she promised. "She will make you jackets and moccasins and smoke your fish and fix your bannock."

"And what about my enemies?" He didn't have any that he knew of, but it was good to find out about those things, too.

"I'll see they don't harm you," she answered.

He liked that better than what the gray horse had said. His grandfather had always told him to be wary of a spirit that spoke of revenge. A man couldn't trust that kind of a spirit-helper. It was better to get one who was not so eager to harm.

Before the spirit left, Marvin promised to summon her in a couple of nights and give her his decision. He didn't want her to know it yet, but he had already decided. She seemed like just the spirit-helper he wanted. He would try her for a few weeks and find out how capable she was.

87

12

During the next several weeks, as the winter worsened, Marvin did so well that he began to think his new spirit-helper was making a difference. He had eight fine beaver blankets, a dozen mink, and fifty muskrats. As his luck improved, he summoned his spirit-helper often, promising her good gifts for her help.

By this time he was accustomed to the solitude. He could lie for endless hours on his bunk, looking up at the ceiling, or sitting near the stove where he would watch the flames and absorb the warmth of the burning wood. Or he would search the pages of the Simpson-Sears catalog he had brought along, reading the descriptions and prices of articles he had never seen.

If it hadn't been for Ella, Marvin would have stayed on his trap line all winter. His luck was still good, but in late December he finished working his traps and went back to the reserve. He figured Ella would be lonely for him by this time. Maybe she would be lonely enough to be willing to go out to his trapping cabin with him for the rest of the season.

But Ella wasn't waiting for him. She was Velmer's girl now, living with him in a little cabin on the edge of the village, although her smile was still bright for Marvin.

"I really wanted you." Her sensuous young lips pouted. "But it was so long until you were coming back, and I was so lonesome."

"You could go back to my cabin with me," he suggested.

"And leave Velmer?" she said. "He wouldn't like that."

When Marvin saw that it was useless to talk further with her, he stormed away, got drunk, and beat up two of his best friends. Some time after midnight he staggered up to his grandfather's cabin, routed the old man out of bed to finish the night on the floor, and sprawled on the bed himself in a drunken stupor. When he finally awoke late the next morning, he was alone and the cabin was cold.

He sat up slowly, his head pounding and the cold seeping into his body. Dimly he could remember what he had done, and the shame burned in his cheeks. Had anyone else laid a hand on the old man, Marvin would have cracked his skull. How could he ever face his grandfather again?

He went around the village talking to first one and then another until he learned that his grandfather had spent the rest of the night at Beardy's and had been seen at the store that morning. Relief gleamed in Marvin's tortured eyes. He spun on his heel and strode back to the cabin where he harnessed his dogs and left for his trap line. He couldn't face Jeremiah. Not that day, at least. His humiliation was too great, too raw and bleeding.

Back on the trap line he tried to forget what had happened. Now he didn't know whether he even wanted to return to the reserve. But when spring threatened to free the icebound waters of Birch Lake, he began to dream of going home. At last the day came when he gathered up his traps and set out for the village, his sled piled high with furs.

He still dreamed of Ella at night, remembering the warmth of her arms about him and the excitement of her lips. He wasn't too concerned about getting her back, however. When he turned his furs into cash, it would be easy enough to coax her into his arms.

Velmer and Ella were away when he returned to the reserve. They had gone to the Northwest Territories for commercial fishing, and no one knew when they would be back.

Marvin shrugged, surprised that he felt no worse than he did. One girl was as good as another.

During the next two years Marvin was unsure about the value of his spirit-helper. There were times when he called on her that his luck remained consistently bad. He couldn't find a moose or hit one if he did, or his nets remained empty, or he couldn't get any beaver in his traps. When that happened, he swore savagely that the spirits were no good at all, that it was a waste of time trying to have a *Mistabeo* of his own. Then, when his disillusionment was the deepest, it seemed that the help of his spirit would come surging back. When that happened, he got jewelry and cloth to hang in the bush for her.

And all during those two years he did not know her name. "I'd like to ask her," he told his grandfather, "but I've been afraid to. She might get mad and quit helping me."

The old man's head bobbed sagely. His grandson was learning his lessons well.

"She will tell you when she wants you to know. Until then, wait."

Then, in the middle of Marvin's third season on the trap line, a great blizzard choked the trails and the temperature dropped to bone-chilling lows. Days passed when he wasn't able to go outside except to cut another stick of wood. It was not surprising that he ran out of meat and that his supply of flour and macaroni dwindled dangerously.

The day came when he knelt at his grub box, realizing there was scarcely enough food left for a week. He sang the song to call his spirit-helper and talked to her about it.

"I'm just about out of everything. If I can't get some meat, I'm going to have to take up my traps and go back to the reserve. I haven't caught anything in my snares and I haven't even seen any moose sign since December. I've got to get some meat."

"You always bring me nice presents," she told him, a warm smile tickling the corners of her mouth, "and you call me with respect. I'll see that you get your moose before the sun goes down tomorrow."

He was relieved. He always felt better after talking to her, whether anything good came to him as a result or not.

Although he had finished the conversation, the spirit-helper hesitated for a moment, as though reluctant to leave. Marvin eyed her curiously.

"And this is the way I look." With that she turned and her human form dissolved; she became a robin, hopping into the distance and disappearing.

Marvin got his moose the next morning not two hundred yards from his cabin. As soon as he got back with the meat he burned a little sweet grass and tobacco in the Robin's honor. Gone was the memory of all the times she had failed him, crowded out by success. A spirit-helper like the Robin was worth having.

Marvin's trapping luck got better after that, and when he got back to the reserve just before spring breakup, he had more skins than he had ever had before.

His smile flashed when Laraviere complimented him on his catch. It had been a lucky day when he got the Robin as his spirit-helper. He had remembered or forgotten her as the matter of his own good fortune soared or languished, but he was not going to forget her again, he told himself. He was going to see that she got the gifts she ought to have.

"Give me three lengths of cloth," he blurted impulsively.

"Three lengths? You aren't going to hang that much cloth in the bush, are you?"

Marvin squirmed uncomfortably. He didn't want to talk about such things with the white man, even though he was his friend. The Frenchman couldn't be expected to understand.

"Why would I hang cloth in the bush?" he hedged.

Laraviere waddled to the rear of the store where he kept a few bolts of material. "Here's some good cloth. Any girl ought to like it."

Marvin scarcely looked at the material. It didn't make much difference what it was. It was the thought that pleased the Robin. He was glad no one was in the store when the old Frenchman was teasing him. He wasn't ashamed of his spirit-helper, but he didn't want his friends to know about her. He had bloodied more than one nose to stop their laughing at his grandfather because of his *Mistabeo*. He didn't want to go through that again.

There was excitement in the village that spring. While Marvin was still out in the bush, a letter had come in to George Beardy from a young white man in Regina. Beardy read it over several times, pondered about it for a day or more, and went to discuss it with Jeremiah Rabbit Ear.

"What do you think?" he asked when he finished. "Should we let him come to the reserve for the summer?"

Jeremiah tugged thoughtfully at his bony nose. "I don't like it, George. Why would a white man want to come to our reserve?"

"He says that he wants to learn about our customs."

"He wants to come to laugh at us."

The chief opened the envelope once more and read the letter-head aloud. "The North American Indian and Metis Protective Association. He sounds important."

"I still don't like it. He's got to have some reason for coming. He's not doing it for us; he's doing it for himself."

"We shouldn't say that, Jeremiah. We don't know that to be the truth."

"Did you ever know a white man to come to the reserve for any other reason?"

Beardy thought about that, and he had to admit that Jeremiah was right. The white man simply did not come to the reserve without reason — always selfish, as far as he was able to determine. Laraviere was there to help Hudson Bay make money off the tribe and even Emily Bannister had wanted to sway the women and children over to her religion. The young man who was asking for permission to come and live on the reserve for a few months was probably just like the rest. Still, the chief did not like to turn down the request.

"Why don't we go over and see Laraviere at the store?" Jeremiah suggested.

"We can go and talk with him," the chief acknowledged reluctantly, "but the council and I will decide."

The Hudson Bay manager's opinion was the same as that of Rabbit Ear.

"You can do as you please, George, but if it was me, I wouldn't let that character get within a thousand miles of the reserve," Laraviere told him. "He's got to be bad medicine."

"Bad medicine?" The chief's eyes wrinkled. He didn't like

the fact that the Frenchman disagreed with him. After all, he was the chief. Still, Laraviere was his friend and he was courteous to him. "What do you mean?"

"I don't know this fella." In his agitation the Frenchman's voice grew loud, almost belligerent. "I never even heard of him before right now, but I'm telling you that he's trouble — bad trouble for all of you. He's got to be a Communist."

"A — A Communist?" The chief had heard of Communists. He thought he knew something about them, but he couldn't figure out why a Communist would want to visit their reserve, or what harm would come of it if he did. He was only one young man.

Laraviere tried to explain how the members of the Communist Party tried to cause trouble between people who ought to get along. He told how they would make speeches and try to get the Indian mad at the whites.

"They would like to make me your enemy and you my enemy. That's the sort of stuff they're best at. So, the only thing for you to do is to refuse to let him come in here at all."

Laraviere knew it was never wise to try to force his opinion on the tribal leader about matters that concerned the people, but he was so disturbed by the possibility that the young stranger would be allowed to visit that he went against his own best understanding of the Indians and their ways.

In the discussion that followed, the council agreed with the opinion of their chief.

"Laraviere's white himself," they said. "He doesn't like the idea that another white man is going to live on the reserve for awhile."

"He said the stranger's a Communist," Jeremiah protested. "He said he'll only cause us trouble."

"How does he know? Has he ever met him?"

The argument was heated, but in the end the council sent word to Floyd Post that it was all right for him to come and spend the summer at Birch Lake.

13

THE YOUNG WHITE MAN came in on the last cat train of the season, introduced himself to George Beardy, and asked for a location to pitch his tent. He was a quiet, personable young man who showed respect for the Indians. The chief was glad the council had gone against the wishes of Jeremiah and Laraviere.

"He is going to be a good example for our own young men," he told his old friend. "I'm glad he came."

Rabbit Ear snorted. "Trouble. Nothing but trouble."

Beardy's eyes narrowed. "You let Laraviere do your thinking for you."

"And you don't think at all!" Jeremiah got to his feet and hobbled away angrily.

Marvin spotted the green splotch of canvas against the dirty white of melting snow when he and his dogs were still far out on the ice. It wasn't grass, he told himself. It was still too early for that. And it was the wrong shape for a canoe. It looked like a tent only it couldn't be. Nobody on the reserve had a tent like that.

In a few minutes he was close enough to see that it actually was a neat, little tent with aluminum poles. His curiosity flamed. The metal poles revealed that it was a white man's tent. No Indian would use such poles when the woods were full of birch, spruce, and poplar. But what would a white man be doing on the reserve?

"Heeyah!" He snapped the explosive lash over his dogs and

they strained in the harness, jerking the heavily loaded sledge even faster.

As soon as he got home, he asked his grandfather about the strange shelter and the man who lived in it.

"He came." Jeremiah shrugged his personal disapproval. "And after a while he goes away, like the ice in the spring."

Curiosity slid across Marvin's lean features. When there were white visitors on the reserve, they always stayed with Laraviere, a service offered by the Hudson Bay. This man must have come to stay for a time.

"But why did he come? What can a white man do here?"

With effort the old man pulled his gaunt, bony frame erect, watery brown eyes slitting. "He says he is here to learn the ways of our people." The old man snorted. "But he spends his time with the young men who don't know nothing."

The next day Marvin met the white man and Vetel on the path.

"I'm Floyd Post from Regina." His smile broadened as he thrust out a firm, muscular hand. "And I'm glad to know you, Marvin."

"Hmm," he muttered, studying Post's blond hair and eyes the color of the big lake shimmering in the summer sun. He had never seen one with such a light skin and hair, or such blue eyes, although he had seen many white men in the north.

"We're going to get together at my place tonight," Vetel said presently. "Why don't you come over?"

"That's right," Post added. "Come over and have a beer with us."

The broad-shouldered Cree, who stood half a head above his friends, frowned, uneasiness glimmering in his features. "I haven't got paid for my furs yet. I ain't got no money for beer."

"You don't have to have none. Floyd's bringing it."

The heavy muscles about Marvin's jaw tightened. Why would this white man who had never seen him before buy beer for him? To be sure, sharing was the way of the Cree. Their people had always done it. But it was not the way of the white. The white man clutched what he had to his belly and tried to

95

get more. He wasn't going to do anything for anyone unless it would benefit him.

At first Marvin didn't know whether he wanted to go or not, but a guy didn't get such a chance often. And besides, he had been on the trap line for months without so much as a bottle of wine to warm his insides.

He half expected Post to have something to sell, or a poker game with high stakes to get them into, but that wasn't the case. They played poker all right, and the white man beat them most of the time. But he would only allow them to play for matches.

"Then if I beat you," Floyd said, "you won't think I did it to take your money away from you."

When the game was finally over and the last of the beer was gone, the guys drifted off to their homes. Post walked to Marvin's cabin with him. They talked about many things: the luck Marvin had on the trap line, the loneliness, and how good it must seem to get back. Marvin was about to say good-night when Floyd asked him what he was going to do now that trapping was over.

"Laraviere wants me to work for him again," he explained, "but I don't think I'm going to. If I can get my boat and kicker ready in time, I think I'll do some commercial fishing."

"Sounds interesting. Give me a yell when you get ready and I'll help you."

"I haven't got any money to pay for anybody's help. By the time I pay off the store and my grandfather's bill, I'll be lucky to get a couple of barrels of gas."

Post's indignation marred his handsome face. "Who said anything about charging you? A guy doesn't charge his friends for helping them, does he?"

"*Kawin.*" Marvin spoke reluctantly, unable to understand this strange young man. Post was as friendly as Laraviere had ever been, but in a way he acted Indian. He had the same ideas about sharing. Only there was a difference. At times when Post didn't know anyone was watching him, a fierce light leaped high in his eyes. Marvin liked him, instinctively, but on those occasions he wasn't sure he could trust the white man.

"Then I'll come over and help you when you get ready to put your kicker and boat in shape. Okay?"

The next morning Jeremiah asked Marvin if he had met the young white man who was now living in the village.

"*Ehe.*" He didn't have to ask if Jeremiah liked the stranger. He didn't like anybody who could even remotely be considered a threat to the old ways.

"It is not good that he is here," Rabbit Ear muttered. "His kind brings trouble."

Marvin's gaze came up defensively. "I like him."

"But why is he here? That is what I want to know."

The boy did not answer him.

"That is what I ask the council," Jeremiah continued. "Why does a white man want to live on the reserve? And why does he talk about the treaty rights and the way Indian Affairs refuses to give us what's coming to us? He isn't Cree."

"He is our friend."

"Like the fox is a friend to the rabbit."

"You don't know that, grandfather," Marvin countered. "You shouldn't say such things."

But the old man was not to be stopped. "He talks too loud and there is anger in his voice when he tells how his people treated us."

"There is anger in your voice when you talk about it, too," his grandson reminded him.

"*Ehe,* but look at my face. It is the face of a Cree. His face is that of a white man. I have learned never to trust a man who turns against his own."

"That's not being fair."

"Why should all of these things concern him?"

"He wants to help us get our rights."

"*Ehe,* that is what he says, but it is not wise to trust a lynx that barks like a sled dog and wags his tail. He is still a lynx with the teeth of a lynx." Jeremiah's hostile voice shook with emotion. "Our young white friend presses against our legs and licks our hand, but his skin is white and so is his mind and his heart. It is not good, Marvin, to believe all that he says. It can only mean trouble for us if we do."

The old man ate the rest of his breakfast in haughty silence. Marvin was unconvinced, but there was no use in trying to argue with the old man. Jeremiah had decided Post couldn't be trusted, and as far as he was concerned, that ended the matter.

Marvin had to admit that he himself had certain reservations about their white friend. Laraviere had labeled Post a Communist and that was disturbing. He didn't know too much about Communists or why they were so bad, but he had always heard they weren't the sort who could be trusted.

Someone else would have pried into Post's political beliefs with care, trying to keep the inquiry secret, but not Marvin. The thought did not even occur to him. Painfully honest and direct himself, he approached everyone else the same way. When he began to wonder about the white man, he got him alone and asked him.

"Me a Communist?" Post's laughter rang.

"Are you?"

"Would it make any difference if I were?" he asked, hedging.

"Laraviere says you are."

"I believe that every man has the right to be treated decently by everyone else," Post said. "And if he isn't, I think he's got the right to band together and take what belongs to him. Is that so bad?"

Floyd spoke so easily, so fluently that Marvin found himself overwhelmed by the torrent of words.

He took what the white man said to mean that he wasn't a Communist, but the nagging doubts still lingered in the inner corners of his mind.

During the weeks that followed Marvin got better acquainted with the white man. Post helped him tune his outboard motor and caulk and repaint his boat. And when the commercial fishing started, the young white man insisted on helping him.

"But I don't want a partner," Marvin protested again, thinking that was the motive behind his wanting to help. "I like to work alone."

98

"Who said anything about being your partner?" Post echoed. "I just want to help you, unless you don't like to have me around."

"It isn't that," Marvin said. "It isn't that, at all." He just didn't want to share the money he would be making with anyone.

Once that matter was settled, he was glad for Post's assistance. The white man knew a lot about outboard motors for one thing. He even had a tool box and a few parts. And he was a hard worker. More than once he was down at the beach painting the boat or putting new rings in the kicker an hour before Marvin was out of bed.

The tall Indian found that he enjoyed Post's company more than he ever supposed he would. They talked endlessly as they worked, and, as usual, the conversation got around to the injustices in the treatment of the Indians.

"There should have been a hospital with good doctors right here on the reserve," Floyd said when Marvin told him about the death of his mother. "They might have been able to save her life if there had been."

Marvin hadn't realized that before, but the more he thought about it, the more convinced he was that it was true. His mother had been sick for a long time. A good doctor on the reserve would have found that out and started treating her before it was too late.

"And there ought to be a good high school here, too, and it should be run by the Indians. What does a white administrator three hundred miles away know about your problems?"

This young white man knew all about the injustices of the past and the problems the Indians faced at present. When they got home after a long day together, Marvin burned inwardly against all the wrongs that were being done against their people. At times he couldn't even sleep at night.

But he said nothing. There was no use in raging to anyone else about it. They were trapped — held captive by the heavy-handed administrators with their piles of regulations and mountains of forms and carbons. He would have thought that talking with Post about such things would help, but it only increased his frustration and sense of helplessness.

Post spent a great deal of time with Marvin that summer, but he worked with others, too. He seemed tireless. When George Beardy decided to go out into the bush after a moose, Floyd volunteered to go along. He helped skin out the hefty animal, cut up the meat, and helped pack it to the lake where they had left the canoe. He went back alone for the green hide when he learned that George's wife would like to have it to make her youngest son a new jacket. Before that trip was over, Beardy was convinced that the strong, capable young man was truly a friend of his people.

Post helped Vetel, who had come back alone after losing Ella to a Metis storekeeper in the Territories. The Indian's fishing boat had to have a new bottom after being smashed in on a rock and his kicker had developed an ominous knock.

When Post finished there, he overhauled James Rediron's old kicker as well, infusing it with life the Indian didn't know was there, and helped one of the older men cut logs to build a new cabin. When fall came and it was time for him to leave, the entire village was sorry to see him go. Everyone, that is, except Laraviere and Jeremiah who were still set against him.

"He says he would like to come back," Beardy told Marvin's grandfather. "And all of the council, except yourself, are agreed that he is welcome to come and stay on the reserve as long as he wishes."

Jeremiah glared darkly at him.

"The people are all agreed that he is our friend."

The old man exploded. "It is not good to call such a one a friend, George. The men say that because he helps them."

"You act as though he is the same as any other white man, but he wants to help us. Look how he has worked for everyone."

"Sure, he works for us without charging nothing, but we still don't know why he does it, or what it is that he's after."

"I've tried to tell you. He helps us because he is our friend."

"Friend?" The word was spat from curling lips. "You don't really believe that, do you? How could you be so stupid? Every night he has the young men together playing cards and drinking beer. And you say it is good?"

"They drink beer anyway," the chief reminded him testily.

The muscles in the older man's wrinkled face drew taut.

"I keep asking questions, but nobody answers them for me, George. Who is he?" Jeremiah demanded. "Why does he come here and spend his money on our young men? And why does he spend all summer working for us without charging us nothing when he could go anywhere and get a job to earn money? What is he going to get out of this?"

A slow scarlet rose in the chief's bronzed cheeks. He sought for words but there were none.

"Did you ever know a white man to help us without getting something out of it for himself?"

Hastily Beardy got to his feet, bumping the table and knocking it resoundingly against the wall. "I suppose you know more than me and the rest of the council!"

"I suppose I do!"

Still fuming, George Beardy stormed away from his old friend, muttering angrily to himself.

14

MARVIN AND HIS friends missed Floyd Post when he was gone. They missed the excitement of always having something to do. They missed the nightly parties and the poker games and the beer and wine the white man had on hand. And they missed the heady talk of the way they had been abused by Indian Affairs and how they could force the government to give them what was coming to them.

"They give us five dollars apiece at Treaty time and a pound of tobacco for the chief, and we're supposed to scrape our bellies on the ground thanking them for it," Vetel stormed.

"How long's it been since any of us except Marvin has earned a buck workin' for somebody else?" James Rediron wanted to know. "There ain't no work around here for us an' there never has been. The jobs're all saved for the white man."

"Yeh," Vetel added, "and look at the crummy shacks that we've got to live in. When Ella and me were in Hay River, you should've seen the kind of houses the whites up there've got. They were as good as the house the Bay furnishes Laraviere. It's no wonder our kids get TB and have to go out to Saskatoon to the San."

"Like Post said, you don't see the white man livin' in houses like we've got. He just wouldn't do it. And if anybody tried, there'd be big trouble."

Marvin pushed back from the table. "We ought to *make*

Indian Affairs give us all good places to live. They'd do it if we got worked up enough about it to go after them."

"Yeah," James agreed.

"And there ought to be meat for our bellies when we get unlucky and can't find a moose."

"That's right. You don't see Laraviere goin' out in the bush with a rifle to get his meat. When he wants a piece of steak, he goes into the freezer and picks out a good big one and has it cooked for him. The other white men don't have to go out and kill their meat either."

James Rediron's anger surged. "It ought to be the same for us. We shouldn't have to go chasin' off an' hunt moose to keep our kids from starvin'."

Marvin grinned. "What kids?"

"Give me time. Give me time."

Now it seemed that they always talked about such things when they were together. They complained about the lack of work on the reserve and having to take welfare checks and the way Indian Affairs shoved them around. And there was a new bite to their voices.

"The worst of it is that there ain't nothin' that we can do about it. They've got everything stacked against us. And that's the way it's gonna be until we get our backs up enough to make them treat us like people."

"And it's gonna be that way as long as George Beardy's the chief," James went on. "And as long as the old men are the only ones on the council. They're so used to doin' what the white man says that they'll never do anything to get us our rights!"

"George Beardy's been a good chief," Marvin protested.

"He's kept us all slaves, that's what he's done. I was talkin' to Post the night before he left. He said we're gonna have to get all the old men off the council and get some of us on it before we'll be able to do anything about forcing Indian Affairs to give us our rights."

The others nodded in agreement.

"But how're we gonna do that?" Vetel wanted to know. "They've got the people behind 'em."

"Maybe." Rediron's voice reflected a sudden pulsation of ambition and power. "But if some of us stand up to Beardy, we can force him to quit and let me be the chief."

Disbelief gleamed in their eyes. "You?" Velmer exclaimed. "Where'd you get the idea that you could be the chief?"

"Post told me. That's who."

He stood erect. "If you'll follow me, we can make Beardy turn things over to me and you guys can be the council. Then we can go to work. We'll send someone to Regina or Winnipeg or even to Ottawa if we have to and stay there fightin' until we get our rights."

The idea was all right, they argued, but they didn't like the thought of Rediron as chief.

"There's a dozen guys better'n you, James," Velmer muttered.

"Name one!"

The argument raged until James spoke up hotly. "All right! All right! Let's leave it to Post when he comes back. He knows about such things. He'll be able to pick out the one who'll be the best *okimaaw*. Okay?"

"Okay. We can't do any fighting against the white man if we spend all our time fightin' each other."

Marvin felt himself being caught up in the excitement of the moment. Change was in the wind. They were going to get together with the other Indians on the neighboring reserves. United they could make Indian Affairs right their injustices and live up to the Treaty, or even get it changed. It was exhilarating talk that caused a man's shoulders to straighten with pride. Marvin almost wished he didn't have to go trapping that winter. He would like to stay and talk and plan with his friends.

For a time he even considered going back to the store to clerk, but being confined to four walls again and to a job that demanded his presence every day was enough to bring pains to his belly and the haunting look of a trap-caught beaver to his eyes. He was born for the bush, for the clean blue skies and the wind in his face, for the lonely places. To tie himself to a building was enough to take the joy out of living.

So, he went out and patched his trapping cabin, bought a few more traps, and repaired his sled and dog harness.

Mentally he reviewed his trapping success of the past season and the help the Robin had given him. That reminded him that he hadn't bought her any gifts since the end of the fishing season. That afternoon he made out an order for the prettiest jewelry in the Simpson-Sears catalog, a whole six dollars' worth, and two yards of cloth. He didn't know whether it would do any good or not, but it would do no harm to try. He mailed the order and was approaching his grandfather's cabin when someone called out to him.

He spun quickly on his heel to see Samuel Morin running towards him.

"What's wrong?" he demanded, reading the panic in his friend's actions.

"My little girl just lays there. She doesn't move or nothing. Where's Jeremiah? He's got to come quick and get his spirithelper to heal her."

"He went with George to get a moose," Marvin explained. "They'll be gone two — maybe three days."

Marvin was looking past his distraught visitor at a robin sitting on a bush not far away. The Robin! She had promised him the gift of healing!

"Maybe I could help," he said impulsively.

He got the sweet grass and tobacco his grandfather always kept for emergencies and started down the trail, with Samuel hurrying along half a step behind. At the Morin cabin Marvin pushed through the crowd of relatives and friends and into the bedroom.

Suddenly panic gripped him. He had never tried to heal anyone before.

Grimly he took the sweet grass and tobacco and lit a pinch of it on the airtight heater. He held his hands in the smoke, singing the song the Robin had taught him to use to summon her, a haunting, toneless chant that rose and fell in unmelodious cadence like the restless undulating of the big lake in the wind.

Going over to the bed where the motionless child lay, he began to massage her frail body.

At last the little girl's lips parted enough to allow a groan to escape. Marvin stopped singing abruptly. It had happened so quickly that he was frightened.

The women in the fetid bedroom crowded closer. While they watched, even their breathing cut off by the emotion of the moment, the girl shuddered and groaned again.

Marvin began to chant once more, softly, until she cried out a few moments later. Then she looked up, lips quivering, and began to sob.

Samuel came to Marvin as he left the house a short time later and took his hand, tears trembling in his eyes.

Marvin liked the feeling that swept over him, the gratitude in his friend's voice, and the glow of importance. Everyone looked up to George Beardy and Jeremiah. Now they would look up to him, too.

That night Jeremiah and the chief came back unexpectedly, their canoe filled with the meat of two fat young moose. But it was not the success of the hunt that gleamed in the old man's eyes as he faced his grandson.

"You are going to be a big man in the village, Marvin," he said proudly.

Marvin wasn't thinking about the same thing Jeremiah was thinking about, however. The first stirring of ambition and lust for power pushed into his consciousness. James thought he could be the chief if George Beardy was pushed out, but there was no way for him to get the older ones behind him. Marvin wasn't entirely sure that he wanted to be chief, but if he did, he reasoned, what had happened that afternoon would be a giant step towards his being accepted by the people.

"The Thunder spirit told me you would have great power," his grandfather went on. "He said you would give a sun dance for your spirit."

Marvin grunted. He had heard often enough about the religious observance of the sun dance.

"It would please the Robin if you held such a dance in her honor," Jeremiah went on, his voice almost a whisper. "You could make your plans for the time of the new moon in the coming summer and announce it now. That would make your spirit happy and place the council and the chief behind you."

Marvin didn't know why, but his grandfather irritated him. He was the one who had healed the child. He was the one who should get the idea for pleasing his spirit-helper.

A quick rush of anger flushed his cheeks. "I'll take care of it."

"*Ehe*," Jeremiah murmured sadly. "Only don't do wrong by waiting."

Marvin was on the way to the store to pick up the balance of the supplies he would be taking with him on the trap line when a strange aircraft circled and touched down on the water in front of the government dock.

"Know them?" he asked James Rediron.

"Maybe." A smile escaped the other man's lips. "Let's go down and see if I'm right."

They started in the direction of the lake.

"Floyd Post's going to send a plane in for me today or tomorrow. Could be that's who it is."

"For you?" Marvin's scorn was evident in his voice. "Why would he send a plane in for you?"

"I tried to tell you guys the other night, but you wouldn't listen. Floyd and I have got big plans. We're gonna be workin' together."

"That I'll have to see."

"You will." James Rediron's laughter echoed above the hum of the idling motor. "Stick around awhile and you will."

It didn't seem possible, Marvin reasoned, but his companion's voice did have the ring of truth in it.

The plane was not for James, however. It had come to bring in Bruce Norris and his wife for a brief visit.

"You're Marvin, aren't you?" Bruce held out his hand. "This is my wife, Tina."

Marvin wasn't sure how the lank visitor could remember his name. He had only seen him a couple of times and that had been several years before.

"Your grandfather is the one I treated so terribly when I was here the first time."

Tina moved a few steps away, impatiently, as though to end the conversation.

"Can you tell me where to find George Beardy? He's still the chief, isn't he?"

"He's still the chief." Marvin couldn't understand why Bruce Norris would want to see the chief, but it didn't matter to him one way or the other as long as it didn't hinder his going out on the trap line that afternoon.

Marvin was in his grandfather's cabin packing the last of his gear when Bruce Norris stopped by. Jeremiah was scarcely civil.

"There wasn't any use in your coming over here to talk to me," he retorted irritably. "We had our council meeting and decided we don't want any other missionary living on the reserve. Is that clear?"

"I thought perhaps we could talk it over."

"There's nothing to talk about." Painfully, Jeremiah pulled himself erect. He was so curt and unfriendly that Marvin was ashamed for him.

"Well, if you ever get over to Deauval, stop in and see me. I'm the DNR officer there now."

Marvin didn't know why, but he walked back to the store with their visitor. He was curious about Norris. He had understood he was going back to school to be a doctor. Now he was a field officer for the Department of Natural Resources at Deauval. He wanted to ask about it, but didn't dare. A polite Cree would never be so prying.

"I'm sorry about my grandfather," Marvin apologized. "He doesn't like outsiders."

Bruce nodded. "He's got reason enough to be cold and unfriendly with me."

They were silent for a dozen steps or more.

"I told the Mission I'd check for them to see if there was any chance of getting the council to change its mind when their request to send someone in to take Emily Bannister's place was turned down for the third time. I guess they're not ready to change their minds yet. We'll have to pray some more."

Marvin examined the field officer's smooth face thoughtfully. It had been a long while since anyone had mentioned prayer to him.

Before he left Norris at the steps of the store, the officer talked with him about the importance of having a personal relationship with the Lord Jesus Christ and gave him a New Testament.

"I hope you'll read it, Marvin."

He probably wouldn't even have taken the book if it hadn't been for his grandfather's rudeness, but he couldn't treat Norris that way. He shoved the testament into his pocket and hurried back to his grandfather's. He had to hurry or he wouldn't be able to get across the lake and out to his trapping cabin before dark.

15

Marvin went out on his trap line, the acclaim of the reserve still echoing in his being. He had considered staying at home to wait for the others to bring their sick for healing, but he was growing restless once more after spending so much time in the village. He longed for the quiet of the bush, the pleasures of being alone and matching his skill against the beaver, mink, and lynx.

During the endless quiet of his stay in the trapping cabin, he got out the testament that Norris had given him and tried to read it. He was quite surprised to find some of the same stories there that Miss Emily had told them. It was interesting until he came to the parts about sin. When that happened, he quit reading.

He hadn't said anything to anyone except his grandfather about the sun dance, but that winter in his cabin he worked out the details.

His grandfather would help, seeing to it that he knew about all the details that had to be done properly. Having a sun dance wasn't a hurried thing. The plans had to be well laid, with the sweet grass smudges and the pipes being done in the prescribed manner. If it wasn't done right, it was better not to be done at all.

Lying in the darkness of the trapping cabin or sitting alone before the fire he planned the observance in minute detail, building it from the many stories Jeremiah had told him about it.

He could see the rapt faces of the older ones who were entranced by the return of an event they all thought would never again be seen on the reserve. There would be skepticism and curiosity flecking the eyes of the young; but their hearts would jerk them out of the day of rifles, aircraft, and power toboggans to the proud hour when the tribe was a force to be reckoned with and the man with a spirit-helper was powerful, indeed.

Marvin lived and relived the moment when he would sing his power songs and the people would listen in awe that one so young had such rapport with the spirits. Once he held the sun dance, he would become known as a powerful medicine man. They would all look up to him.

For the first time a new ambition kindled and began to burn within Marvin Lacendre. Why should one like Rediron become the chief if Beardy were to step aside? He didn't have the respect of anyone. Why didn't he go after the job instead?

At first the thought was so absurd that he laughed aloud. How could he ever be the chief? He hadn't even had a name until Laraviere helped him make one up.

But he had the respect of the people, and especially the older men. They would get behind him in a way they would never get behind James Rediron. He would be able to do something for the Cree to right the wrongs that had been done against them by the whites.

When he thought about such things, Marvin got so excited it was all he could do to keep from jerking up his traps and going off in search of Post to tell him his plan. Together, he and the white man would be able to set things right.

The fact that Post might have committed himself to backing James did not occur to Marvin. He was the better man. Anyone would agree to that. So, he was the logical choice to take old Beardy's place.

Closing his eyes, he tried to study out what it would be like to be the chief. He would have to get the people behind him first. He had already made progress in that direction by healing Samuel's little girl. And when he held the sun dance he would take another long step.

Then he would have to convince the men that something

could be done about their problems. They already talked about the injustices. He had heard them talk about the days before the white man when there was plenty of moose and caribou for everyone and the lakes and rivers were filled with fish. He didn't know how many times his grandfather and Beardy had longed, almost tearfully, for the day when a man could snare beaver and mink and wolves to clothe his women and his children as well as himself.

It had been a good land in those days, they said, except for the Chipewyan who came to do battle now and again — a land where a Cree stood proud and tall, the master of his own destiny.

And then they would recall the day when the round eyes came, their skin as pale as birch bark or the belly of a jackfish and their dreaded rifles loaded and ready for battle. They talked of honor and truth, of being fair in the way they treated the Cree, but their lips spewed lies. They made treaties and broke them and made treaties again, calling the Indian brother while they killed off his moose and caribou and stole his land, forcing him ever farther back into the rocky lake country of the north.

The Indian knew all of those things. He just had to be reminded again and again until he could see that he had to stir himself to action. Winnipeg and Ottawa would listen if the people were disturbed enough to go and speak to them.

That was Marvin's plan. He would work on the leaders of the reserve until they were ready to move. Then he would be able to accomplish something for them.

Before leaving his trapping cabin that spring Marvin realized something else. It wasn't only for the sake of power and position that he wanted to be the chief of the reserve. Those things were important, it was true. But more important, being chief would give him the opportunity to help his people.

With the help of Post perhaps he could have a small part in helping to remove the dejection and helplessness that enslaved them. It was a heady purpose that quickened his pulse and made him tremble.

His mind crowded with plans for the future, Marvin took up his traps as the snows disappeared and went back to the village.

He expected everyone to be as excited about his return as he was himself, but when he saw their indifference he felt forgotten. Post had come back briefly, capturing the imagination of the young men and stirring the old by the words of the past, the aching memory of injustices long and painfully recalled. They said the same things Marvin was thinking, only their words were harsh and their tone belligerent.

The young men liked what they were hearing. It was all right for the old ones to sit by the fires nodding their heads and moaning about what had happened to their fathers' fathers. The flames burned high in the blood of the smooth-cheeked young. Although seldom voiced, until now, their resentment against the white man had smoldered within like the smoky burning of the peat beds for months or years after fire had blackened the forest above. But now their anger was finding voice in the tempestuous words of the white man and his Cree protégé. There was excitement in the village over Post's return.

"He and James went out to Prince Albert to meet a black man from America," Velmer said. "He's going to tell us what we can do to make the government give us what we ought to have."

"A black man?" Marvin had heard about such people. He had even seen pictures of them. But he had never supposed he would get to see one with his own eyes. No wonder the people on the reserve were excited.

There was no use in talking about the sun dance now. No one would hear him.

Marvin didn't like the way things were going, but a plan was beginning to form. He would wait until Post and James and the black man came back to the reserve. It would probably be best to wait until after the newcomer had spoken, so there would be nothing to claim the white man's attention. Then he would convince Post that he would make a much better *okimaaw* than James. That might take some doing, but it could be done. He would have to get Post to talk to the older men, those who were in positions of authority. They would tell him about Marvin's position with the people, his ability to heal. And, if he had to, he would tell him about his spirit-helper and the sun dance he was going to have. That ought to convince him that Rediron wasn't the one to back.

Everyone in the village met the aircraft when it circled and touched down on the wind-scarred surface of the lake. They stood in silence on shore, the sun glittering on their bright jackets and skirts of red and green and blue. They were all excited by the coming of their strange visitor, but that was not revealed in their stoic, impassive faces.

The village could rock with laughter, but it seldom did before strangers. The Cree were too well-mannered, too shy and reserved to show emotion before those they didn't know.

Post was the first to get out of the cumbersome Norseman aircraft. The stranger was next, a lanky individual with a twisted smile, his hair as woolly and rounded as a porcupine and skin no darker than their own.

"He's not a black man," Velmer whispered. "He must be Indian."

Marvin said nothing. The stranger didn't look black to him either. The talk about the stranger's color must not have been true.

While he was staring curiously, James Rediron climbed out on the float, pride showing in every move, and turned back to the plane in an affected gesture of ownership. As if on command a bright smile and flashing brown eyes appeared in the doorway.

Marvin gasped! And so did half the young men in the crowd. There was a girl with James! A girl with a strangely familiar face.

She reached down for his outstretched hand and jumped lightly to the dock, her cotton dress showing a generous expanse of thigh. Well aware of the excitement she was creating, she smoothed out her tight-clinging dress, pulling it down over her hips, and glanced up at James.

"Look what he picked up," Velmer murmured.

"That's Aldina Brouilette," somebody else observed. "You remember her."

"Nobody like that *ever* lived around here."

"I don't care who she is," Velmer continued. "All I hope is

that she stays at home when he goes running around the country with Post."

"If she does," somebody else retorted, "you'll have to wait in line. Half the guys in the village will be over to see that she doesn't get lonesome."

Marvin sucked in a deep breath. The girl was Aldina Brouilette! He would have recognized her anywhere!

16

Post ushered his black guest off the dock and introduced him to the intense young men who were standing shyly to one side. "This is Ray Otis."

Marvin remained motionless on the fringe of the curious villagers. Although the white man gave every indication of being unhurried, he moved steadily in the tall young Indian's direction.

"And this is the one I was telling you about, Ray," he said, respect flecking his eyes.

The stranger's glance was cold and critical. "You ought to be able to bust somebody's guts and make him like it."

Ray Otis felt the muscles in Marvin's powerful right arm and stepped quickly away. "Don't worry. I ain't takin' no chances with him."

Marvin squirmed. He knew Otis meant what he said as a compliment, but it still bothered him.

Post had made arrangements for Otis to stay at the chief's house. Beardy was the most important man in the village. It would mean much if he could be won over to their cause, and the black man was one who just might be able to do it. On the way Otis gave instructions to the others.

"Now, remember, we've got to talk different to the chief than we do to the young turks in the village who're already spoiling for a fight. We've got to persuade him that we're the only ones who can give him the help he needs to get a fair deal from the white man." He paused, glancing at Marvin as though trying to determine whether he could be trusted or not. "These old codgers are plenty smart. It takes more than words to light a fire under them."

Marvin was studying the stranger just as intently. Gone was the gutter talk and rough language. The fire in Ray's voice and the wild, impassioned stare in his eyes had both faded away.

"Why did you come here?" Marvin asked abruptly.

The black stranger stopped, the friendliness in his dark features giving way to hostility. "What did you say?"

"I asked why you came here. What do you care about us? It doesn't make any difference to you whether we're treated right or not."

"It should make a difference to everybody that you're not given your rights. If you don't get your rights, how are my people going to get ours?"

"Don't get so shook up, Marvin," Post broke in. "Otis is as concerned as I am about your people. That's why I sent for him to come up and help."

"We've all got to stick together in this thing," Otis continued. "If I come up and help you, we'll be able to overthrow the white man and his government together. That's why I'm up here helping you."

"Otis!" Post spoke quickly, the warning signals in his voice. "You're getting carried away again. We aren't talking about overthrowing anybody's government. We're talking about treaty rights.

Ray's laughter was as thin as the afternoon air. "That's right. I guess I get so upset when I think about the injustices the people here have had to put up with that I get to thinking the whole system ought to be kicked out."

"That's exactly right," Velmer put in. "We've got to show 'em they can't get away with what they've been doin' to us. The only thing they understand is force!"

Marvin wasn't sure he liked that kind of talk, but he said no more. Otis was a guest and he had come to help them. It wasn't polite to be critical.

Ray's attitude towards him seemed to change. He asked his advice often and insisted that Marvin accompany him on his visits in the village. "I'd like to have you see what I tell the people so you'll know what to say yourself when we start using you."

"I guess I can go with you," Marvin murmured, trying to keep the stranger from seeing how pleased he was. He was sorry now that he had ever doubted him. Ray seemed truly concerned about the people and he was tireless in his efforts to enlist support.

Marvin learned much about the way to persuade people to action. Even more important, he was beginning to build himself a reputation with Post's first assistant. Ray would be able to help him against James Rediron when the time came.

The black American's message changed from one house to another. When he was with the older men, he talked about the treaties the white man had not lived up to and about the right of full and free medical services on the reserves. He talked about better schools under complete Indian control, the need for more economic development on the reserves, and money to make badly needed improvements. He talked about the game that used to roam the forests and about the lakes that were filled with fish and the towering piles of fur they used to bring in from their trap lines. The things he said were logical and intelligent, the orderly listing of grievances. And his solution was as intelligent and as orderly as his presentation.

"We're going to bring those days back," he assured them with the quiet gentleness of a statesman. "We've got to organize the Indians in Canada so they can speak in Ottawa with a single voice. Then the government will listen. They will have to."

"Hmmmm." Tears came to sunken, faded eyes, tears mingling with a hope that had been dead for more years than anyone could remember.

In the homes of the younger men the American's language was bitter. "The white man isn't going to give you anything. He takes your moose and your furs and your women and what does he leave you? A crust of bread? You can trap the squirrels if you want to, when they've taken the mink and the beaver." He swore savagely. "We're going to change all of that if we have to burn 'em out to do it!"

118

"What do we have to do?" they would ask, hot-eyed and eager to be at it.

"You've all got to get together first. Then you've got to fight, baby." Hatred rang in his voice.

"You've got guns," Ray said. "Start getting all the ammo you can lay your hands on and squirrel it away somewhere. You'll be needing it before we're through!"

"We ain't got much money," someone told him.

He fixed a scornful gaze on the man who dared to voice a protest. "Doesn't Indian Affairs give you ammo?" he demanded. "They're supposed to."

"They give us enough to kill a moose once in awhile. Anything more than that we've got to buy."

"The Bay's got plenty of money," Ray countered. "And they've stolen furs from your people for three hundred years. Bust in and take what you want. You've got to learn to stand up for your rights!"

The old way Marvin's grandfather longed for had laws against stealing and lies and selfishness. This Ray Otis didn't want to live by either the laws of the Indian or the government. He seemed to want to make his own as he went along.

Marvin's shoulders came back and his spine straightened. In spite of all those things, what the black American said was true. Even his grandfather and Beardy would agree to that. Marvin glanced about the little cabin where seven or eight intense, fiery young men had gathered to listen to Ray. He saw the same pride he felt gleaming in their eyes.

After several more days of visiting in the homes of the people and talking to small groups of men wherever he found them, Ray said the time had come for the speeches. He and Post got permission to use the council house, which was used for the meetings on the reserve. But when the people began to gather, it was apparent there would not be room for everyone inside.

They shuffled towards the council house, converging lines of gay colored blouses and jackets shimmering in the sun. Others from outlying cabins came by kicker-propelled canoes, entire families crowded into the sleek, gray crafts.

Excitement on the reserve was infrequent, and the appearance of Floyd Post and Ray Otis caught the imagination of the people. It was a gay, expectant crowd that gathered at the council house, crowding the building and overflowing to the grass outside.

Post was the first to speak. He thanked everyone for coming and had a special greeting for all of his old friends. Then a serious note crept into his voice as he explained the purpose of the meeting.

"On Ray's side of the border it is the black man who is held under the government's heel, along with the Indian," he thundered. "It is the black man who is showing the way by shaking off the last shackles of slavery and taking that which belongs to him."

He paused, and when he began again his voice was hushed with emotion. "Now your black brothers are offering to help you do the same."

"Hmmmmm." The sound rippled across the crowd.

"The Black Power of America holds out its hands to the Red Power of Canada in a common fight to overthrow the system and gain freedom . . . ."

He went on, but to Marvin his words were suddenly a jumble of sound. Aldina had joined the crowd a few feet to his left, eyes fixed raptly on the speaker. So intent was she in listening that she was not aware of Marvin. As for him, he had completely forgotten that Post was talking.

There was much about Aldina to remind him of the girl who had left the reserve to go away to school. Her long braids, pulled forward over her shoulders and shimmering as black as night against the clinging softness of her sheer cotton dress, framed the comely line of her cheek and her delicately formed nose and mouth. She was so much fairer than those around her that he might have doubted her Cree heritage had it not been for the ebony of her braids and her deep, clear brown eyes, pulled slightly at the corners to set her apart from the round-eyed whites. There was an appealing little-girl quality about her smooth face and the unashamed way in which she wore her dress, as though completely unaware of her provocative figure.

Slowly Aldina became aware of his presence, of the fact that he was looking at her. Her eyes shifted to his handsome young face, and the little girl became a woman. A brazen smile lifted the corners of her full, red mouth and her eyes whispered invitingly to him. He felt a kindling desire within his body that was not altogether unpleasant although it made him think of his mother. He had seen her look at men in that same way.

"Marvin," she said, her smile deepening.

"I didn't think you'd remember me, Aldina."

"How did you know who I am?"

"I'd never forget you."

She pouted impishly. "Don't say that. When we were kids, you didn't even know I existed."

"That shows how stupid I was."

"You could make up for it now," she said softly.

"But you're Rediron's girl." What he really meant was that she was living with James, but he couldn't say it right out, although he didn't know why. Possibly it was because of his mother and the sort of life she had lived.

"Only he's gone all the time."

Grinning, he touched her bare arm just above the elbow. "A pretty girl like you shouldn't be lonely."

The speeches continued and Marvin said no more to her, but later, when Post and Otis asked him to join them in Rediron's place, he refused.

"You'd better think it over. It could be a big deal for you," Post said.

"That's right. We've been talking it over, and we've both agreed that you're our man," Otis added.

"If you work hard and do what we tell you, you can be the *okimaaw* here at Birch Lake." A strange grin twisted the white man's face.

Marvin was slow in answering. It was what he had been longing for — what he had wanted more than anything else in the world a few short weeks ago as he thought things out in his trapping cabin. Now, however, he wanted something else even more.

Let Rediron run around from one reserve to the other. He'd stay in the village and keep Aldina from getting lonely!

17

ALL THE YOUNG MEN and most of the old came down to the dock to see Post and the others leave. A few paces away Jeremiah Rabbit Ear watched, disapproval glinting in his watery eyes.

"Waaci."

He didn't have to look up to recognize the owner of the voice.

"What do you think of them?" Laraviere asked.

Jeremiah did not answer. He didn't care to talk to his white friend about the visitors. As far as he was concerned, James Red-iron didn't count. They had him on a leash like a dog, and he barked when they told him to.

The Frenchman repeated the question.

"Their words were pleasant to the taste," Jeremiah said.

His old friend stared at him, incredulous at first. Then understanding gleamed in his squinting eyes. "But they grip the belly like too many blueberries."

Jeremiah looked away uncomfortably. He didn't like it when someone read his thoughts. It made him feel naked and defenseless.

"There are many who think so," he countered. "There are those who find their words as sweet as honey."

"If I really thought they wanted to help your people, I'd be for them in spite of the things they're saying about the company I've been working for, for the last forty years. But I don't trust them."

Jeremiah had to admit there was truth in what Laraviere was saying. He had been suspicious of the white man from the first, but had been even more disturbed by the newcomer. There was hatred in Ray's voice and a wild hatred in his eyes. And the old man didn't like the careless talk of burning and killing. Such speaking stirred up the young men and could only lead to trouble.

As he went back to his cabin, Jeremiah was greatly disturbed. Reason told him to be wary of the strangers, but his heart responded to the things they had said. Questions tumbled, unanswered, in the inner recesses of his mind. Men often came with the voice of the songbird and the deceit and intentions of the wolverine seeking to spoil and destroy. If he wasn't so robbed of strength these days, he would have another conjuring lodge and ask the Thunder spirit about Post and Otis.

He caught a glimpse of Marvin and disappointment wrenched him. If his grandson had only held the sun dance, he would probably be ready to try a conjuring tent himself. He wanted to talk to him about it again, but Marvin didn't come home that night until after Jeremiah was in bed, and when he got up the next morning he claimed he didn't have time to talk.

The old man was grumbling about it as Marvin snatched a piece of smoked fish from the table and walked out, eating as he went. He could have talked with his grandfather, he supposed, but he had stopped by James Rediron's house twice the night before and Aldina hadn't been there either time. He was determined to catch her that morning before someone else got to her. Half the guys on the reserve would be making a path to Rediron's door.

James lived on the opposite side of the village, a short distance and a few trees separating him from the nearest neighbors. Marvin stopped and wiped off his mouth with the back of his hand. Although her mother still lived in the village, Aldina had moved into Rediron's cabin.

At the door Marvin paused, nervous for the first time. He knocked lightly, but no answer came. He waited for a moment before rapping again, a little louder. There was still no response. He was about to hammer on the door once more when a sleepy voice from inside the cabin called to him.

"Yes? What is it?"

"Aldina."

Another long moment of silence and the door creaked open. She was wearing the same dress as the day before, only now it was wrinkled, and blood veined her eyes. Apparently she hadn't been lonely for James very long.

"You could've come in," she murmured. "The door wasn't locked."

"Is James home?"

Her smile teased him. "If you came to see him, I'm disappointed."

That told him all he wanted to know. He stepped inside and closed the door behind him.

"I thought maybe you'd already married one of these nice, good little girls who curl up their noses at me," she said.

"Not me. I've been waiting for you to come back."

She sat down on the side of the bed and pulled him down beside her. In a way she was glad he wasn't married. In another way she wished Marvin had a wife and a raft of kids at home. She would have found real satisfaction in luring him away from one of those women who gossiped endlessly about her.

"They think they're so much," she blurted. "I'm as good as they are."

He stared at her questioningly, already forgetting what they had been talking about.

"Oh, forget it," she muttered petulantly.

Aldina liked him. He was sure of that. And she enjoyed his visits. At least she always urged him to come back.

But he wasn't the only man who came to visit, carrying a bottle of wine or cheap whiskey, a couple of boxes of cigarettes, or a scarf as a gift. He wasn't the only one who urged her to move into his cabin with him either.

When James came back towards the end of the month, he stayed so close to Aldina the few days he was home that no one else had a chance to be with her. That seemed to be the way she wanted it. Wherever he went, she was at his side, clinging possessively to him.

The young men came down to talk to Rediron while he was in the village, eager to learn how the trip had been going. Marvin was there, too, but not because he wanted to hear what James had to say. He came only because Aldina was there.

"What do the people say on the other reserves?" Vetel wanted to know. "Are they with us?"

"*Ehe.*" Rediron's entire being seemed to glow. "And they are behind me as *okimaaw,* too."

Aldina beamed, tightening her grip possessively on her lover's arm.

"They're all going to be with us before we're through," he said. "We'll have the whole Cree nation in our hand. And when we get that, we're going to force the government to give us our rights! They'll be scared not to!"

"How are we going to do that?" Marvin broke in, contempt showing in his voice.

"When we're banded together, we'll force them to give us everything we want!"

Marvin frowned. It was easy to understand why Aldina hung on James the way she did. He was an important man these days. Still, it was good just to think about all the wonderful things that were going to happen when they began to win their rights.

"What did you do on the trip?" someone asked James.

Pride jerked Rediron's shoulders straight and a smile proudly appeared on his lips. Aldina, too, was smiling, drawing honor from her relationship with him.

"At first I listened, but towards the end I gave some of the speeches myself."

Disbelief gleamed in their brown eyes.

"Ask Post when he comes back," he retorted defensively.

"He might lie for you," Stanley put in.

"I tell you I made speeches," Rediron retorted, anger building in his voice. "Two or maybe three times I talked and Post said I did better than Otis. He said that the people would listen to me because I'm Indian."

Velmer's grin widened. "Give us your speech, if you're so good."

James stared briefly at the speaker, color darkening his cheeks. "A guy's got to have people to speak to."

"What're we?" someone asked.

The chorus went up gleefully. "Give us a sample. Let's hear what you have to say to them."

He kicked the floor with his moccasined toe. "I — I don't know if Post would like it."

"We won't tell him."

Marvin, who was sitting near the back, studied Aldina's somber face. This was going better than if he had planned it. The guys were making a fool of James right in front of her. She was seeing him for what he really was, a liar and a braggart, a phony. She would soon know that he could not be the chief of the Birch Lake Reserve or any other, if she didn't know it already.

Aldina caught Marvin looking at her and her cheeks darkened. She knew well enough what he was thinking and anger flecked her eyes. It wasn't that he thought James the fool that bothered her. It was the reflection that fell on her. She never had been able to stand ridicule.

"Go ahead," she urged, lifting her voice. "Give the speech like you did at Pine Lake last week."

He got to his feet. "You guys won't tell Post, will you?"

"He won't hear nothing about it."

That seemed to satisfy him. He cleared his throat and began.

The laughter died in the mouths of the scoffers. Rediron was speaking very well. Maybe he wasn't doing better than Ray Otis, but they could better understand what he was saying. He used stories of bear and wolverine and beaver to explain what he meant. Before he was half through an illustration they would be nodding in agreement. He was caught up in the force of his own words and spoke passionately.

Doubt turned to bewilderment as the little group of listeners realized that Rediron had, indeed, spoken before audiences. Their bewilderment turned to awe. He had the power within him to stir men's hearts. When at last he finished, the little cabin was charged with emotion. They stared at him, stunned by the force of his oratory.

Marvin wilted inside and almost died. What chance would he have against James now?

126

Those who listened to the speech had pledged themselves to silence, but the story was too exciting to remain a secret. By the time Post returned the entire village knew it.

"You come to speak to all of us?" the chief asked James.

Horror clouded Rediron's face. "I only speak when Post asks me to."

But that was the wrong thing for him to say. The chief and one of the councilmen met the white man at the dock and asked him about having Rediron speak. The white man was delighted.

Marvin groaned in silence.

"I'm proud of you, James," Post said loudly enough for all to hear. "From the first time I saw you, I knew you were the man the people would all want to follow."

Marvin could not even sleep that night for thinking about what had happened. Rediron's fame was spreading beyond his own on the reserve. He was losing the opportunity for power and position, and at the same time he was losing Aldina. She would never leave James to go with him now.

He was a better man than a dozen Redirons, he stormed. Why did James have to get everything?

Marvin didn't know why he hadn't thought of the Robin before. She had promised to get him the girl he wanted.

Only that had been a long time ago, and he hadn't called on her for so long that he couldn't remember the last time. She might be angry because of his neglect.

For the space of half an hour or more he considered the matter. If it were something less important, he wouldn't even bother asking his spirit-helper. But at that instant he had to have Aldina or he no longer cared to live.

He couldn't understand why she meant so much to him. She was so much like his mother had been that there were times when he cringed at her actions. It might have been that very similarity that caused him to be so captivated by her, but whatever it was, he knew that he had to have her.

Quietly he pulled on his pants and moccasins, rummaged through his gear until he found the sweet grass and tobacco which he kept handy but hadn't used for months, and shuffled outside.

As he ignited the smudge, he began to chant the song she promised to hear and answer, his voice rising and falling on the still night air. Before he finished it the second time she appeared in his dream, a mocking smile on her face.

"*Waaci.*"

The tone of her voice was disturbing. His grandfather had been right when he warned him to be careful about giving gifts to his spirit-helper or she would get mad at him.

"Should I know you?" she asked.

He cleared his throat and wished he had remembered about the cloth and the jewelry.

"It is a long time since I called on you," he said lamely. "And I'm sorry for that."

"I listen for you," she scolded, but I do not hear you. I go out to the bush where you hang my gifts, but I see no new ones. Only the old are there, rotting in the sun."

"I'm going to get you nice gifts as soon as I can. They have to come from Eatons or Simpson-Sears."

Her face softened to the extent that a smile rested lightly on her lips. "And now there is something you want," she told him. "Something that means much to you."

"*Ehe.*" He felt better, but not good. She still hadn't said she would grant his request, but she hadn't refused.

"You know Aldina Brouilette?"

"I know her."

"I want you to get her for me."

For a moment it seemed that the Robin frowned and Marvin shivered. That wasn't a good sign. It wasn't good at all.

"If you do, I'll give you two yards of cloth," he blurted.

The instant he did so, he realized two yards of cloth would not be a suitable gift for getting him such a one as Aldina. For a moose, maybe, or a good night at cards, or a good week on his trap line, the cloth would do. But not for such a one as Aldina.

"And I'll get some beads and bracelets and rings," he added quickly, lest the Robin get so angry she turn her back on him and he lose out altogether. "I'll get some beads and bracelets and rings

128

and put them in the bush for you — so many you won't be able to wear all of them."

That seemed a little better, but still she did not reply. There had to be something else he could do to persuade her to get James Rediron's woman to come to his cabin for good. The Robin might like to have a beaver blanket or a couple of good mink pelts, but he had sold all of his furs and would have no more until he went trapping again in the winter. It would take another gift even more important to her than those.

The sun dance!

Why not?

"I'll give a sun dance in your honor next June or July?"

He waited, eyes narrowing and muscles rigid with emotion, stretched to the breaking point. The Robin was studying his gaunt face, her own expression still unchanged.

She was weighing the matter, trying to decide whether to do as he asked or not. He wanted to shout that she had to help him. He was about to speak once more when a new light gleamed in her eyes and her lips parted. He leaned forward, eager to catch the sound of her voice. Suddenly her smile flashed once more. She waved to him and disappeared from his dream.

18

THE CHILL FALL WIND bit through Marvin's light jacket, but he shrugged it off. There was no use in going back to the cabin now. He wouldn't be able to sleep. He knew no more about whether the Robin would help him get Aldina now than he had before he talked with her. He had asked for her help, but he didn't know whether he was going to get it or not. He should have known that he couldn't neglect his spirit-helper and not suffer for it. Aimlessly he paced the village paths until the early morning sun awoke the dogs and set them to yelping.

Marvin had no intention of telling his grandfather about the matter, but the instant he entered the cabin Jeremiah sensed something was wrong.

"Do you have troubles?"

"Nothing I can't handle."

There was wisdom and discernment in the old man's faded eyes. "It's with your spirit-helper, isn't it?"

Awe etched itself on Marvin's face. "How did you know?"

Jeremiah shrugged. Actually, he had heard his grandson get up and rummage in his gear for the sweet grass and tobacco before going out into the night. Listening at the window, he had heard him singing the song to call the Robin. But there was no use in letting Marvin know everything.

"The Robin might be angry with you," Jeremiah said. "And she might be teasing you."

"You think so?"

"Ehe."

Marvin curled his fingers about the cup of tea he was drinking. "What should I do?"

The old man smiled bleakly. "Get some gifts from Laraviere and put them in the bush for her. Let her know that you're not going to forget her any more."

He studied the matter carefully. "Only I don't have any money until I start trapping again."

"Talk to Laraviere. Tell him you'll pay him later."

Marvin didn't say anything to his grandfather, but the manager of the Bay hadn't been too anxious to let him have the last order on credit.

"What're you doing with your money?" the Frenchman wanted to know. "You did good fishing."

"Ehe." He had done well fishing. He always did.

"Have you been giving all your money to Post and that wild man, Ray Otis, like everybody else?"

"I — I kept most of it for — for other things."

The Bay manager laughed. "Like that 'adopted wife' of James Rediron's, eh?"

Marvin's cheeks stained, and he started to gather the order from the counter quickly so he could be on his way.

"You don't need to get so shook up about it. Everybody on the reserve knows you're one of the ten or twelve guys who're keeping her entertained while James is away making the white man let you have Canada."

Anger suddenly flecked Marvin's eyes and he spun on his heel. When Laraviere started on something he didn't know when to quit. That had been a full week ago and he hadn't been back to the Bay since. He wasn't sure whether Laraviere would extend him any more credit, even for something so important to him.

Velmer was glaring at the Hudson Bay manager across the counter, fists clenched and anger staining his dark cheeks.

"We've got to have some grub."

"You should've thought about that before you started giving all your money to Post and Otis." The storekeeper laid a coil of garlic bologna on the counter and wiped his hands on the front of his grimy shirt.

"I always pay you back."

The manager was riffling through the smudged credit cards. "Let's see, Velmer. You owe the store $139.00 and you haven't paid anything on your account for almost three months."

"As soon as I start trapping, I'll pay you."

Laraviere's eyes snapped. "You aren't a trapper."

"I'm fixin' to trap this year."

"You'd better if you want to keep on charging here at the store. You're up to your credit limit right now."

Still Velmer did not leave. "My little girl is so hungry she cries."

What d'you expect me to do about it?" But even as Laraviere complained, he was taking items off the shelves. Macaroni, flour, and lard enough to last a week. And before shoving the sack to- wards Velmer, he dropped a little bag of candy in it. "Take this stuff and get home with it. And see that Alice gets those candies."

Appreciation gleamed briefly in the Indian's eyes. It wasn't easy to have to come to the Frenchman and beg for everything. He'd be glad when Post and James got them what was coming to them.

"I'll pay you soon."

The manager dismissed him with a wave of his hand. "Forget about paying for this order. I'll do that myself. But if you get any money, put it on your bill so I can start charging to you again."

The wind was roaring out of the north, piling the swells high on the open lake and hammering breakers against the dock. The bite of winter was in the air. Traffic into the reserve and out of it ceased as it did twice every year at freezeup and breakup.

It was a time of soaring bills at the Bay and, for many, short rations. The commercial fishing money was long since spent and the trapping hadn't started.

This year the situation was even worse than usual. Post came back to the reserve about the time the fishing checks were being cashed. No one knew how much had been given to him or taken in for him at the meetings they held.

"We've got to visit all the reserves in the western provinces," he explained, "and that means we've got to fly."

And everybody knew that flying costs money.

The men tried to keep Laraviere from finding out about it, but he knew almost before the plane came back for Post and the others.

"I guess it's no different than spending their money on rotgut and gambling and women," he told Jeremiah, "but I've got a little book with the names of the guys who've been giving this Post character their money. There's going to be a payday one of these days."

He let Marvin have the gifts he wanted for the Robin, but not before he gave him a stiff lecture about giving to the white man.

"You give him any more money, Marvin, and you're through getting credit here. Understand?"

But Marvin had the gifts he wanted, and that was all he cared about at the moment. It was not the custom of the Cree to worry about the future.

Besides, he knew the old Frenchman well. He would grumble and snort and stomp the ground like a bull moose at rut, but in the end he would give him the stake he needed to go trapping. He guessed Laraviere figured that was the only way he would ever have a chance of getting his money back.

It seemed to him that Aldina's attitude toward him began to change from the day he put the Robin's gifts in the bush. She gave him preference over all the others, even when he didn't have any money to buy her gifts.

"I tan this moose hide to make moccasins for James," she said, giggling, "but I think I'll make them for you instead. How about that?"

He picked up one corner of the skin, examining it with experienced fingers. It had been carefully fleshed and tanned.

"Only don't tell James where you get them."

He put his arm about her and drew her down to his lap. His joy was boundless. He felt as though he ought to take the moc-

133

casins and hang them in the bush for the Robin, only he would never dare do that. Aldina would expect him to wear them. They would be more than moccasins to him. They would be a symbol of his coming victory over Rediron. All the way back to his grandfather's he sang the song of the Robin softly, to let her know how happy she had made him.

Laraviere was a stubborn man and as cunning as the wolverine. By listening, he was able to learn who Post's most ardent supporters were. They, of course, would be the ones who were giving the largest sums of money. He had already threatened to cut off the credit of those who helped the strangers, but he had to have some examples to frighten the rest.

He chose them with care, younger men who either weren't married or had no children who would suffer. Let them feel the sting of his disapproval and they might not be so eager to hold Post's handkerchief when he sneezed.

The first skim of ice was forming on the bays when he cut off the charge accounts of half a dozen of the youngest, most hotheaded followers.

"I only need a stake to go trapping," Stanley said plaintively.

"Why don't you write to Post? Tell him your belly is empty and see what he says."

The young Indian's temper exploded. "You buy the furs I bring in and you take the bill out of the money before I get any."

The manager's rasping voice had a raw, jagged edge. "How do I know you'll even be trapping? There ain't one of you who wouldn't bust a gut to go with Post if he asked you."

Resentment smoldered ominously in the silent Indian's eyes.

"You young bucks've got to learn who your friends are."

Laraviere didn't like doing it, but he had to protect them, he reasoned. In a couple of weeks the bite would be on so savagely that they would know Post and Otis were the cause of their troubles.

The young men got mad and pounded on the counter when they realized the old Frenchman was not to be swayed by pleading. They stormed at him, faces flushed and eyes hot with anger.

But that only strengthened his conviction that he was making progress in his campaign to discredit Post.

"You're only one," they reminded him ominously. "And look how many we are, if we decide we have to come and take what we need."

"There's always the RCMP to take care of guys who steal," he reminded them.

"We're not scared of them," Stanley blustered, spitting his contempt.

The store keeper was disturbed. He had never heard talk like that from them before, but he couldn't let them know it. "Before you steal from this store, you'll have to get by this rifle." He jerked his head in the direction of the moose gun on the wall in his office.

He tried to tell himself there was no danger, yet change was in the wind. Change he could not entirely understand and wasn't sure he could cope with. A year — six months before — and they would not have raised their voices against him.

That night as soon as he closed the store he waddled over to Jeremiah's to find Marvin, but he wasn't there.

"Tell him I've got to see him as soon as he comes in. I don't care what time it is."

Jeremiah didn't think his grandson would do whatever it was Laraviere wanted him to, but he would leave the telling to him. He had been acting strangely the last few weeks — since before he talked with him about his spirit-helper. It was probably that Brouilette girl he was seeing over at Rediron's. The old man didn't like having Marvin hang around with a girl like that. She was too much like Betty. But there was nothing he could say to change him.

Jeremiah laid awake until Marvin came stumbling in so he could give him Laraviere's message.

"I don't feel like seeing him tonight," he mumbled, alcohol slurring his words. "I'm sleepy. I'll see him tomorrow."

19

STANLEY AND THE OTHERS didn't go back to the Hudson Bay store during the next week, and Laraviere began to relax in spite of the fact that Marvin refused to sleep at the store to guard it.

"I've got to get my traps ready," he explained lamely.

Actually, that wasn't the reason. It was Aldina. He was finally making progress with her, and he didn't dare do anything that would cause him to lose ground again. She wasn't the sort who would sit home alone at night, and he couldn't be with her and guard the store at the same time.

He didn't mention the job offer to her, but she learned about it and it pleased her to know he preferred being with her to working.

"I wanted to be with you," he explained when she asked about it.

"That pleases me." She bent impulsively and kissed him lightly on the lips.

"You could be with me all the time," he said huskily.

A pixie grin brightened her face. "That would be sort of nice. I always have liked you."

"I know where I can get a little house."

"James will be home next week."

He studied her face quickly to see if Rediron's return was going to interfere.

"I'll wait to move in until he leaves, okay?" There was a question in her voice, a gentle probing.

"He'd just as well know it now."

She laid a hand on his wrist. "Will you keep him from hurting me?"

The next morning Marvin made arrangements to rent the house he was thinking of, agreeing to trade two of his best beaver traps for two months' rent.

It mattered little on the reserve that Aldina moved into a cabin with Marvin. He had been calling regularly enough on her and staying long enough to give him some sort of priority as far as her affections were concerned. So it was not surprising that he was next on the list.

Stanley and a couple of his friends challenged Marvin about it, however.

"James is out workin' for us and what do you do? You steal his woman?"

"I just said, 'Come on, honey,' and she came."

"He ain't gonna like that," Stanley retorted. "An' Post ain't gonna like it neither."

Marvin jerked erect, eyes flaming. "Post ain't her father. He's got nothin' to say!"

"You've worked for Laraviere!" his accuser continued. "You don't care nothin' about the rest of us!"

Something exploded within Marvin. His massive hand snaked out, caught Stanley by the jacket, and hauled him close, lifting him until only his toes touched the ground.

"I ought to pound you into the sand for that!"

"I didn't mean it!" Stanley blubbered fearfully. "I didn't mean it!"

Contempt overwhelmed Marvin. He flung the man to the ground savagely. Stanley remained there until Marvin turned and stalked away, his face hot with anger.

In the store a few minutes later Laraviere called Marvin into the back. "A radio message just came in for Stanley. Seen him around anywhere?"

Marvin grunted.

"Rediron and Otis are coming back." The Frenchman's lips trembled. "Some of the guys must've sent for them."

"I don't believe it."

"Read this QSO."

He took the paper and read the radio message.

"They're coming to cause trouble," Laraviere continued. "I've felt it in my bones!" His lips quivered and his cheeks were ashen. "The first time I saw that Post I ought to've had him thrown off the reserve!"

Marvin started. Laraviere must have the same opinion of him that Stanley did. He was talking to him as an ally, a traitor to his own. It was a kick in the belly.

"You'll stand guard for me tonight, won't you?"

"*Kawin!*" He spat out the refusal angrily as though that would help to cleanse the hurt from his soul. "If our people took everything you've got in a thousand stores, we wouldn't begin to get back what's been stolen from us in the last three hundred years."

"Marvin!" Laraviere cried, more in pain than in anger. "Not you too. *Not you!*"

Stunned by the anguish in the Frenchman's voice and the burning rage of his heart, the young Indian pivoted and stormed outside. He pushed past a woman on the path, bumping her with his shoulder and forcing her to step out into the loose snow, but he was scarcely aware of it. Stanley and the others were still together somewhere; he was sure of that.

He found them an hour later, seated around the table in the cabin that belonged to one of them. Without knocking he pushed the door open and bent through it.

Stanley pushed back from the table, fear glazing his eyes. "I don't want no more trouble with you," he muttered.

"You'd better get over to the store. There's a QSO waitin' for you."

Resentment glittered in Stanley's eyes. "Did Laraviere send you to find me?"

Marvin's lips curled. "To have you get this message? Don't be stupid. He'd sooner throw it in the stove! But he's got his job to do."

"Is — is it from Post?"

Marvin glared at him. "Why don't you go over and find out?"

138

Post did not come, but Rediron and Otis caught a ride up to the Birch Lake Reserve with the ski-equipped Canso bringing in supplies for the store. Laraviere came out on the front steps and stared as the young Indian men who had sent for help came down to meet the two men. He swore loudly enough for a dozen people to hear him.

"Troublemakers! Swine! Somebody ought to throw the whole rotten bunch in jail!"

Marvin waited uneasily while the tight little group closed about the new arrivals and guided them up the path in the opposite direction from the store. There was the matter of Aldina that had to be settled. He would have to meet Rediron before he left the reserve again. Marvin was prepared for that, but to have the confrontation in front of Otis would be a terrible breach of manners.

When he went back to his cabin, Aldina was there waiting for him. "James got here, didn't he?"

His gaze met hers. "How'd you know?"

"I saw him."

"Haven't you got anything better to do than look out the window?"

"You're jealous, aren't you?"

"I just don't want you looking at anyone else, that's all."

She put her arms about his neck and looked up at him tenderly. "I finished the moccasins for you this morning."

His spirits soared. James was back, but she was giving the moccasins to him. That little act told him that everything was going to be all right. Aldina was his.

In the cabin Otis leaned forward, both hands on the table and anger burning hotly in his eyes.

"The white man isn't going to give you anything he doesn't have to. Just remember that. He's using loaded dice in the crap game of life."

"Hmmmm." They weren't sure what he meant, but it sounded like something they could agree with.

"There's no use going to Indian Affairs and asking them to give you enough of what they stole from you so your babies don't have to go hungry. They don't care."

"That's right," Rediron broke in. "They ain't gonna listen."

"They've got their ears plugged with rabbit fur."

Laughter rippled across the group. Otis allowed himself a brief smile before continuing. "You freeze yourself trapping mink and beaver and the white man doesn't even give you half what they're worth." His voice grew harsh. "All you get out of it is enough to buy grub to go trapping again. I say it isn't fair."

"What can we do?" Stanley demanded. "That's what we asked you back for. We want to know."

The speaker's voice was a hoarse whisper. "You've got to stand on your own two feet and take it away from him. You've got to burn if he don't give you what you ought to have!"

Vetel pulled in his breath with a queer, sucking noise.

Otis heard it. Deliberately he fixed his angry stare on the young Indian. "What's the matter with you? You scared?"

Vetel licked his dry lips. "I'll do anything anyone else will."

The black man let his gaze drift slowly from one pair of hate-inflamed eyes to the other, pleased with what he saw. At first he had wondered if these quiet people could ever be aroused enough to assert themselves. Now he was encouraged. They were getting angry. They wanted action. This was only the beginning.

"You've got to be tough! You've got to take what's yours even if you have to use a gun to do it!"

"Hmmmm."

"You've got to destroy the whole rotten system before you're going to get what's yours."

There was almost continuous murmuring now, liberally sprinkled with profanity.

"There's no use looking to the old men," Ray said. "They've been brainwashed for so long that they don't even think for themselves. You've got to take over or there won't be nothing done."

"How do we do that?" someone complained.

"Yeh. They won't even listen to us."

The black man's remark was barbed. "They aren't going to listen until you make them."

As the exhilarated young men listened that afternoon, it was as though the Black American drew aside a curtain to show them the new order of things. They were going to get the land and the gold, silver, uranium and oil, and the lumber and pulpwood. The game and fish would belong to them, too. They would all have plenty of money for everything they ever wanted.

"And before you're through, you'll have the white man's money, his fine cars, his houses, and his women."

"Somebody else'll have to get a woman for Rediron," Stanley jeered. "Aldina's livin' with Marvin now."

Rediron swore above the ribald laughter.

He got drunk that night on money borrowed from Ray and lurched over to Marvin's to make Aldina go home with him. Marvin saw him coming and met him at the door.

"Looking for somebody?" He spoke mildly enough, but his feet were wide set, as though braced for a blow, and his fists were clenched.

"I've come to get Aldina." James staggered forward a step or two, his manner menacing. "And you'd better not try to stop me if you know what's good for you."

Marvin laughed easily. "You've had too much moose milk. You'd better go home while you can."

James thrust out his jaw belligerently, but did not move closer. "Don't you tell me I'm drunk."

Aldina chose that moment to open the door and step out into the cold night air. "Hello, James."

The sight of her brought a drunken smile to his lips. "I knew you wouldn't leave old James for good. I've got a couple of bottles in my grub box and there's more of it around if that ain't enough. Come on home with me."

"I — I can't." She drew back as though suddenly afraid. "He won't let me."

That triggered the attack Marvin had known was coming. James swung at him, his fist moving with surprising speed to catch Marvin a glancing blow on the chin.

Marvin exploded. Bellowing his rage, he coiled and sprang forward, throwing his great arms about his adversary. James flailed

141

at him with both hands, but Marvin ignored the rain of blows and with relentless power crushed him against his chest like a giant bear. As the pressure increased, Rediron's fists were useless and he was fighting desperately for breath.

Suddenly Aldina was terrified. "Don't, Marvin!" she screamed. "You'll kill him!"

But Marvin squeezed James even tighter in his deadly grip until the other man's face began to darken.

"Marvin, stop!" She beat on him with both fists and tried to pry his arms from about the weakening Rediron.

At first her efforts were useless, but at last reason returned to Marvin. He stopped choking James and with a powerful thrust sent him hurtling backwards. The smaller man stumbled over a log and sprawled on the snow.

"Now get out of here!"

"I'm goin'," he mumbled. "I'm goin'."

When James was gone, Aldina touched Marvin's arm hesitantly. "I — I was so scared." This time her fear was genuine.

Angrily he faced her, still staggered by the horror of what he had almost done. "You ought to've been scared. You made him jump me."

Her lips pouted. "That isn't a very nice thing for you to say."

He grasped her roughly by the arm and pushed her ahead of him into the cabin. "Don't you ever do that again!"

20

THAT NIGHT THE ROBIN troubled Marvin's dream, disappointment lurking in her luminous eyes. He knew the reason even before she spoke to him.

"You said you were going to give a sun dance in my honor."

"*Ehe.*"

"Who is that on the bed beside you?"

He did not answer.

"Do you think you would have been able to get her away from Rediron without my help?"

"*Kawin.*" He wasn't sure about that, but he didn't want to argue with her in case she was correct. He tried to think of a quick excuse for not having started preparations for the sun dance.

"I'm waiting," the Robin whispered.

"When I come back from trapping," Marvin promised, "I'll make plans so I can have the sun dance in June at the time of the new moon. It will be the biggest sun dance that's ever been held on the Birch Lake Reserve."

Her manner softened. "That will make me very happy."

The next morning Aldina was still asleep when Marvin got up, and she was eating breakfast when he came back several hours later.

"Is James gone?" she asked.

He dropped to a chair beside the wood-burning heater. "They caught a ride on a plane to LaRonge."

She seemed surprised. "And he didn't even come to say good-by."

Marvin swore.

Her smile was taunting. "Know something? Your ears get pink when you're mad."

He felt like cuffing her.

"If I'd known James was going, I'd have gone down to tell him good-by."

"Shut that blasted mouth of yours and get me something to eat."

"*Ehe,* Pinky."

He snatched a wrench from the table and slammed it at her in one quick, violent motion. She dodged nimbly and it thudded into the wall across the room marring the rough wood.

"You do that again and I'll go with James and never come back!" She slapped him savagely, leaving the imprint of her hand on his dark cheek. "Pinky!"

Marvin leaped to his feet and snared her with both hands. She struggled to free herself and for one desperate moment her fear surged back. "What're you trying to do, kill me the way you almost killed James?"

The anger went out of him as he saw her terror and he pressed his lips against hers. She responded fiercely, clinging to him.

"I don't *ever* want another man," she whimpered.

Marvin knew that was not the truth, but it made him feel good just the same.

Marvin was somewhat surprised when Aldina actually left the village and went out on the trap line with him. Somehow she didn't seem like the sort of person who would be content with the lonely life of a trapping cabin. But she helped him pack their gear and grub on the sled and harness the dogs. He was surprised at the skill in her tiny hands. Her eyes were as bright and expectant as those of a child at Christmas. His heart was singing as they left the village for his trapping cabin across the lake.

Aldina seemed to enjoy it, too, working his traps with him as expertly as any man. She could make a set to fool the wiliest beaver and caught more rabbits in her snares than they could eat. She helped him cut up the moose he shot and carry the meat back to the cabin. And she insisted that he go back for the hide so she could tan it and make him a new beaded jacket.

She was happier than he had ever known her to be. The blood cleared from the whites of her eyes and her smile was softer and gentler than before.

Only the Robin disturbed him. In the late winter she began to appear in his dreams. She came silently, her eyes somber and the corners of her mouth turned down. She must be angry because she didn't think he would keep his word, he reasoned. Maybe the other spirits were laughing at her because he did not give her the sun dance. That would be enough to make her angry.

Lying on the bed at night, still shaken, he planned to talk with Aldina about it the following morning. He would start while she was fixing breakfast, he decided. That would give him time enough to explain why he had to have the sun dance and what it would mean for him.

The people had forgotten his healing of Samuel's little girl, but they would remember when he began to plan for the sun dance. It would make him an important man on the reserve with those who counted — his grandfather, George Beardy, and the rest of the council.

He had promised the Robin her sun dance more times than he could remember, but now he was going to have it. He wasn't going to push it aside again.

But when morning came and Aldina began to chatter to him, he decided to wait until a more convenient time to talk with her.

A few days later he came in from cutting wood for the fire to find Aldina reading the testament Bruce Norris had given him.

"Where'd you find that?" he asked, stiffening against the blast of scorn that was sure to come.

But when she spoke there was a new tone in her voice. "I found it on the floor behind the bed."

He made no further comment, hoping she would think it had been left there by someone else.

"It reminds me of Miss Emily," she continued. "I wonder where she is now."

He shrugged. "The last I heard she had come down with the

sickness of the lungs and had to leave, and the council wouldn't let anyone else come to take her place."

"Remember the stories she used to tell us?" Aldina giggled. "I was fascinated by some of them. Remember the one about that little man. What was his name?"

Marvin built up the fire and sat down. He didn't know why she had to bring that up now.

"You remember that story, don't you, Marvin? This little guy wanted to see Jesus so bad that he climbed a tree so he could look over the crowd, and then Jesus went home to have supper with him."

He nodded.

"And the story about the shepherd with all the sheep except one safe at home, and how he went out to look for that one sheep. I used to ask her to tell that story over and over again."

He remembered that, too. He even remembered reading it for himself after Norris gave him the testament.

Aldina read on for several minutes without saying anything more. At last she looked up.

"You know, Marvin." A wistful note stole its way into her voice. "I don't think I'll ever forget that story of the sheep. When Miss Emily told it with the cloth-covered board and pictures, I used to think that I was the lost sheep she was telling about. I'd feel so bad that I would cry inside, and when I went home at night, I couldn't sleep. I used to wish and wish that Jesus would find me."

He got his dwindling supply of tobacco and rolled a cigarette for each of them. Aldina pulled the warm smoke deep into her lungs.

"If it hadn't been for my mother, I think I'd have become a Christian that summer before I went away to school. I sure thought a lot about it."

"I'm glad you didn't."

Anger came slowly to her eyes. She ground the cigarette into the wooden floor and glared at him.

"What do you mean by that?" she demanded testily.

146

"Nothing, except that you probably wouldn't be here with me now if you had."

She jumped to her feet, her temper blazing. "You're just like everyone else! You want to go to bed with me, but you don't think I'm as good as the other women in the village!"

"I didn't say that."

"It's what you meant!"

It was two or three days before she would let him close to her again. If she read the testament after that, it was when he was gone, but he didn't mention it again. He didn't want to take a chance on igniting that explosive temper again.

Reluctantly Marvin and Aldina watched the snow rot in the warming sun, and they both knew that the time to go back to the reserve was fast approaching.

"I don't want to go back," she whispered, her soft fingers touching his arm, "ever."

"We can take our traps and furs in and go out with the nets in a few weeks," he told her. "There are plenty of places we can fish."

"*Ehe.*" The mood vanished. "But I've been so long without a bottle of wine."

They went back to the reserve two days later.

Marvin had not thought about the trouble between Laraviere and the younger men while he was on the trap line. Surprisingly enough, it was still building. The men had gone off to their trap lines and that had postponed the difficulties. It might have ended then had the trapping been good that season, but only Marvin and Aldina brought in a good catch of skins. The others were scarcely able to pay their loans for traps and supplies.

James and Otis had been visiting in the outlying cabins during the long winter months. When the men came dragging in, discouraged and ill-tempered, they were already blaming Laraviere and the Hudson Bay Company for their lack of money.

Usually the wily Frenchman was sensitive to the mood of his customers and bent the regulations to make them fit the needs of the reserve. But the influence of the strangers was growing stronger, he decided, and he still had to teach the young men that they couldn't go off on the road Post and Otis wanted to take them without having trouble.

Marvin hadn't been back long when he realized that a strange, shadowy tension had wrapped itself about the village; it was like the chill that seemed to come off the muskeg at dusk or a place like Thunder Hill where the spirits forbade men to go.

The activities of the village continued as usual. The trapping season had ended, and the men looked forward to the opening of the bays and the stirring of the big lake that would soon signal the breaking of the ice that held it in bondage.

When Marvin came back to the cabin after selling his furs, Aldina's eyes were bright and her cheeks flushed with alcohol.

"I had company while you were gone," she announced defiantly. "Stanley stopped to tell me that James is going to be back tomorrow."

"Just remember what I told you," he warned. "I'd better not catch him hangin' around here!"

"If I want to see him, I will!" she retorted defiantly. "There's nothing you can do about that."

He took off his parka and sat down. She was drunk and wanted to argue with him. He didn't have to worry about James coming to see her as long as he was around. James and his friends were all afraid of him.

"What's he coming back for?"

"The men are all having trouble with Laraviere," she informed him, stumbling over the words. "Post is sending James to get things straightened out. He's going to make the Bay give credit to all of 'em!"

Marvin snorted. "That I'll have to see. Laraviere won't pay any attention to James. He never has."

"You can laugh if you want to," she snapped, her belligerence growing, "but you'll see. James is a big man now. He's gonna be the *okimaaw* here at Birch Lake and maybe over *all* the Cree reserves. He's gonna help Post and Ray throw over the system and get what's comin' to us." She paused, a silly grin twisting her usually pretty face. "It would be real nice to be the woman of the chief. I could show those gossipy women that I'm just as good as any of 'em. Who knows? I may just move back with James?"

"You do and I'll kill him!" he muttered darkly. "I'll kill both of you!"

Aldina snarled her disgust, but said no more about James. She had seen Marvin wild with rage on one occasion, and she was afraid he might do what he threatened if he had enough provocation.

James Rediron returned to the reserve the following day and the cloud of foreboding deepened. As Marvin moved about the village, he realized that it was the talk that was causing the dissension. Wherever he went there were young men in groups of two or three, heads close together and voices as low as the buzzing of bees. There was a change of attitude, an awakening from lethargy or sleep. He caught it in the snatches of conversation he overheard on the paths as the old men began to talk again of fighting for their rights. He detected it in the tone of their voices when they mentioned Indian Affairs, the RCMP, or even Laraviere.

There were those who said little against the old Frenchman. He was white, it was true, but he had spent so many years among them that he was almost a Cree himself. When George Beardy caught a boy of twelve writing "Death to Whitey" on the wooden steps of the store, he stopped him angrily.

"Clean that off!"

"I didn't mean nothin'!"

"Clean that off!" And Beardy stood over him until he did. "Don't let me ever catch you doing that again. Y'hear?"

Marvin was excited by the change in the people. It kindled his own ambition to be a leader among them and to help in whatever was taking place. He tried to find James and Stanley to volunteer his services, but they were nowhere around. After a day or so he decided they were avoiding him. He supposed it was because he had taken Aldina from Rediron — that and the fact that he had worked at the Bay for awhile.

He went to the store on several occasions, but Laraviere wasn't the same either. He seldom laughed, and Marvin saw that he had taken the moose rifle from its rack and kept it in the corner within easy reach.

"What're you going to do with that?" he asked, indicating the gun.

Laraviere squinted. "Shoot me some wolverines."

"There ain't no wolverines around here."

"You never can tell." He reached back and fingered the barrel.

That night Marvin was almost asleep when a brilliant glow filtered through the murky window flooding the room with a grim, flickering light. Instantly he jerked awake and got up, stumbling to the window.

"Aldina!"

The fright of his voice woke her and she sat up, trembling violently. "What is it? What's wrong?"

He turned from the window. "It's the store! It's on fire!"

21

But it wasn't the store, Marvin discovered, as he dashed to the door and flung it open in order to get a better view. It must be the barrels of gas brought in by cat train during the winter and stored outside some distance behind the building. The flames were leaping higher than the trees, casting eerie shadows.

"What's happening?" Aldina cried.

A barrel exploded as they left their cabin, and a terrified scream ripped the night.

Marvin's blood chilled. Aldina had boasted that James Rediron had come to put a stop to the trouble between Laraviere and the young men on the reserve. This had to be his doing!

It was what the whispered conferences had been about. It was the cause of the tenseness, the foreboding. Icy fingers squeezed at his chest until he could not breathe.

"The rest of those barrels could go any time!" someone shouted.

As though to punctuate the warning, another and still another exploded noisily with fierce bursts of new flame. Aldina cringed against Marvin, drawing strength from his massive shoulder and his powerful arm. There was no use in trying to fight the flames. They were beyond control now. All they could do was wait and hope they didn't reach the store.

"Where's Laraviere? Anybody seen him?"

"Laraviere!" The cry went up.

Marvin looked about quickly, trying to find the old store-keeper's bulky figure in the crowd. Suddenly he sped for the store building.

"Don't leave me!" Aldina cried, but he didn't even hear her.

The door was ajar, as he suspected, and one of the windows was broken out. On the other someone had printed, (using a bar of soap as a pencil), "Burn, Baby, Burn!"

"Laraviere!" he shouted.

The store was a shambles. The cash register had been thrown on the floor and broken open. The radio was a mass of metal and wires, damaged beyond repair, and the old Frenchman's desk had been overturned.

"Laraviere!"

A faint sound drifted to him from the opposite side of the store. He found the old man lying on the floor, groaning and clutching his battered, bloody head.

"Laraviere!" Marvin knelt beside him.

"Look out!" a desperate cry came forth from outside. "The whole place is goin'!"

Immediately another barrel exploded, showering the back of the store with burning gasoline.

"Someone's in there!" a woman shrieked in terror.

Marvin struggled to lift the corpulent Bay manager. Sweat clung to his trembling arms and his broad shoulders. His knees quivered and it was all he could do to keep them from buckling.

Thick, acrid smoke was filling the burning building. It pinched his throat and lungs until he fought savagely to breathe. He forced himself towards the door step by faltering step. Once or twice he stumbled and almost went down, but he managed to stay erect until he was within a few feet of the door. There was a loud cracking sound and the floor gave way beneath his left foot. He lunged forward, his leg buckling beneath him.

Marvin battled to remain conscious, setting his teeth against the pain. The nausea came and went, building slowly, wave on wave. He knew he had to get out of the burning store with Laraviere. The pain tore at his belly until, mercifully, the blackness swallowed him.

Marvin did not know until later that he had tried to crawl forward, pulling the old Frenchman along with him, or that George Beardy and three others found them just inside the door and got them out of the burning building an instant or two before it collapsed.

The people, shock dulling their eyes and drawing color from their cheeks, parted silently to make a path for those who were carrying Laraviere and Marvin. They took them into the Hudson Bay house and laid them on the bed.

Aldina pushed through the growing crowd in the house and made her way to Marvin's side. Tears came to her eyes as he groaned and stirred restlessly. His leg was broken and he was badly burned. His hands were blistered and a triangular piece of skin had been lifted from his forearm when someone tore his shirt sleeve away.

In the other room Laraviere was lying motionless and unconscious on his bed, his breathing shallow and sweat moistening his broad face. Both Jeremiah and Beardy had looked in on Marvin first, but now they turned their attention to the Frenchman. He was more badly hurt than the younger man. There was an ugly gash on the side of his head where something heavy must have fallen on him, and his pulse was rapid and uneven.

Men and women crowded silently into the bedroom to stare at this one who had lived for so long among them. In that moment they realized that they loved him and that he had loved them.

"Can you heal him, Jeremiah?" Beardy asked.

"Indian medicine is for the Indian sickness." He shrugged his own helplessness.

Bewildered and desperate the chief sent for the village midwife to look at both of the injured men. She protested her own incompetence.

"If they were having babies, I could take care of them," she said. "But, no babies — " She shrugged.

"Look at them!" George roared.

She went to Laraviere first, threading her way into the bedroom. There was a thin line of blood at least two inches long with an ugly knot around it. Already the discoloration and swelling had spread down his cheek. His jacket had been ripped at the seam revealing a huge black bruise on his shoulder and his lips were puffed and bleeding.

"He sleeps," she said softly, as though the sound of her voice would disturb the badly injured man. "It is not good that he sleeps with a blow on the head."

"*Ehe*," the chief murmured, still unable to comprehend what had happened. Laraviere had been like a brother to him. They had fought, even as he and Jeremiah fought. They had cursed each other violently, and days had passed when they refused to speak. But now that the Frenchman lay so still and white on the bed, all their difficulties were forgotten. All he could remember were the good things, like the time Laraviere gave him food for his family one whole winter when the snows were bad and he could not get out to work his trap line. And another time when he brought flour over to the house so they would have something to eat, waiting until after the fishing was over for his money.

"He has to have a doctor right away," the midwife said.

"You have a power toboggan," he told one of the men. "We will take him to Deauval."

"*Kawin!*" the gray-haired woman retorted quickly.

Beardy whirled, eyes blazing. "I am your chief, woman! Do you dare to tell me no?"

"He needs to stay here. Send someone to Deauval to radio for the ambulance plane, but leave him here where he is warm and still. It is better."

The anger left the chief's eyes as suddenly as it had come. "What you say is good."

"All the gas is gone, George," someone else said.

"We will have to send someone with dogs then."

By the time Vetel had his dogs hitched and was ready to leave, Marvin was conscious and informed them that he wanted to go to Deauval.

"There's no doctor there."

"The DNR field officer can fix my leg."

"You'll come back walking like your grandfather," Aldina informed him in disgust.

154

"Norris will fix my leg good."

Beardy could have kept him there to wait for the ambulance plane, but he was mindful of what Marvin had done.

"You can take him," he told Vetel.

Marvin was on the sled and they were ready to leave when Beardy came shuffling out to them.

"There is no need to send the message for the ambulance plane," he said heavily. "Laraviere is dead!"

Marvin gasped. "Dead? He can't be!"

But he read the truth in Beardy's sadness and closed his eyes against the sudden pain. No one had ever had a better friend than the old Frenchman.

"Be sure to get those messages to the RCMP and Indian Affairs, Vetel," the chief warned.

Beardy was always careful to follow the rules. It would do the Mounties little good to come out and investigate a tragedy like this. No one would tell them anything. In the case of wife beating, perhaps, or rape, or assault against another Indian, witnesses would step up to be identified. But this was white against Indian.

Vetel shot his whip forward with a smooth, even motion of his arm, cracking the lash like a rifle over the head of the lead dog.

"*Maaca!*" he sang out on the still, cold air. "*Maaca!*"

It would be easy going until the trail swung north and they would have to leave it for a narrow, twisting path through the bush that was seldom used and was often clogged with dead falls that would have to be cut away with an ax. While he could make good time he moved his whip methodically, the sharp staccato of the lash punctuating his own profane shouting to the dogs.

Vetel reached Deauval shortly before noon the following day, his dogs exhausted and his own powerful frame gaunt from hunger and exertion. He drove his dogs directly to the field officer's house and went to the door.

Bruce Norris's wife, Tina, wrinkled her nose when she saw who was there.

"I'm sorry, but I'm afraid I can't do anything for you." As

unobtrusively as possible she reached up to lock the screen. Bruce said she shouldn't be that way, but she couldn't help it. She was always uneasy around these people, and especially when her husband wasn't home.

"My cousin hurt his leg," Vetel continued, mixing the gender of his pronouns in a way that was common to his people. "I think maybe she broke him."

"Come back in the morning and I — I'll send a QSO for the air ambulance."

"*Kawin!*" He spoke firmly. "My cousin, he say the field officer will fix his leg good."

Tina flushed. The people came to Bruce for all sorts of help and advice, as though he could do anything.

The dark-skinned young man who stood before her spoke with the conviction that Bruce could care for his friend. But how could they know of her husband's medical training?

"Your friend needs a doctor," she insisted coldly. If this got started, they would be coming at all hours, and she and Bruce would never have any time alone. "Come back in the morning and I'll have the plane sent over for him."

"I will come back and see the field officer," he informed her.

She was closing the door when Juli came in from the other room and asked curiously, "Who was it, mommy?"

"Just a man wanting to see daddy." She took her four-year-old daughter by the hand in an effort to quiet her own uneasiness.

Bruce came in before dark, weariness etched on his sun-reddened face. He had found the remains of a caribou cow and her calf up-river and the telltale evidence that a white man had done the shooting. He had been following leads since morning without success.

"I'm so beat I finally came home." He dropped into an easy chair in the living room, taking the tea Tina had made for him. "Anybody come around since I left?"

She did not answer him.

"Was there anybody here to see me, Tina?" he asked loudly.

She busied herself in the kitchen, pretending not to hear.

"Daddy!" Juli called from the bedroom. "Daddy!"

156

"You're supposed to be asleep, young lady."

"There was a man here to see you today. Mommy talked to him."

"Okay, honey. Go to sleep now." He closed the bedroom door and then walked into the kitchen.

"Why didn't you answer me when I asked if anyone had been here?" he asked accusingly.

"The radio was closed when he came, so I told him to come back in the morning and I'd send for the air ambulance."

"What's the matter? Is someone sick?"

"An Indian man came over from Birch Lake with a friend who has a broken leg."

Bruce's gaze, hard with anger, found hers. "And you didn't have him bring the man in?"

"I couldn't have him in the house. You weren't here!"

"Tina!" he exploded. "The man is hurt!"

Her temper blazed crimson in her cheeks. *But he's just an Indian!*

He was unable to speak for a moment, but when he did the anger was gone. Only a deep, wrenched sorrow remained.

"I'm ashamed of you!"

She recoiled from the words as though he had slapped her. Tears trembled on her eyelashes, tears of frustration and humiliation and anger.

Bruce grasped her by the shoulders, the hardness coming back to his eyes. "Get the front bedroom ready. I'm going after him."

"You aren't going to bring him into *my* house! Fix a place for him in the office or the garage."

"Get the front bedroom ready!"

22

Back at the Birch Lake reserve George Beardy and Jeremiah Rabbit Ear went about the preparations for Laraviere's funeral mechanically. He had no family or relatives that they knew of and not even any close friends outside the reserve.

"He never got any letters," the chief observed.

"Why should he?" Jeremiah was stunned by his white friend's death. "His friends were here."

Beardy nodded. He, too, was feeling the loss keenly. "Have you chosen a place for his grave?"

"*Ehe*. In the center next to the place where I'll be buried."

The old chief tugged at his pipe. "I will have the place on the other side of Laraviere saved for myself."

Jeremiah was pleased with that. Laraviere would have been pleased, too. It would have given him much satisfaction to have his grave in such a prominent place. It would have showed him how the people loved him.

Presently old Rabbit Ear grasped the edge of the table and pulled himself painfully to his feet. "Why did they do it, George?" he asked. "Laraviere never hurt nobody."

"That is true. He was our friend."

Jeremiah gulped. "The young men liked him, too."

"Then why did they do this thing?"

Jeremiah was long in answering. "It was not them, George. It was Post and the black man and the things they told the young ones to excite and anger them."

The chief tamped tobacco into his pipe. "We, too, are to blame."

"We told them it was bad to listen to such men," Jeremiah countered. "We warned them."

"*Ehe*, we warned them, but we found what they said pleasant to the ears. Secretly we welcomed their anger and hoped it would help us to gain what we all have wanted for so many, many years."

Jeremiah sat down again, arthritic fingers crabbed about the head of his cane. In a way it was so. Everyone on the reserve wanted to be free of welfare and the stupid regulations of Indian Affairs. Everyone wanted the Cree to be master of his own fate once more. Yet he felt no guilt over what had happened to Laraviere. He had always been opposed to the strangers and their wild talk. Even before the old Frenchman had expressed his own anger at Post and Otis, he had been afraid of them and warned Marvin against listening to their honeyed words.

"Has anyone seen James Rediron since the fire?" he asked abruptly.

"*Kawin!*" Contempt honed the chief's voice. "He hides like a rabbit in the bush until he feels it is safe for him to come back to the village."

Jeremiah nodded. His own opinion of young Rediron matched that of the chief.

"He couldn't have started the fire himself, could he?" Beardy asked.

"James? Hah!" Jeremiah's voice rasped. "Would a field mouse attack a lynx?" Marvin might do such a thing if he was provoked enough. He would never have struck out against Laraviere, but he had the capacity for violence. But not James Rediron. He lacked the stomach to face the lake when it was rough.

"And he thinks he can become the *okimaaw* of our reserve," Beardy said sorrowfully. "He would be a sad choice to lead our people."

"*Ehe*. But he could not get the support to be chief now. Even the young ones are turning against him."

"Now they turn against him in their shame," the chief retorted sagely. "But he talks good, and as the weeks and months pass, they may forget. It is that time we have to fear."

Jeremiah's bent fingers tightened about the cane and concern glittered ominously in his sunken, watery eyes. Beardy spoke the truth about the people. Now they knew what James was, but would they remember when the memory of Laraviere and how he had died began to fade.

"What can we do, George?"

The chief's voice trembled. "I have dreaded the coming of this day, Jeremiah, but I have decided that it can no longer be pushed aside. It is time for a new chief to take over. I have stayed too long on the job."

Jeremiah gasped. "You mean you are going to quit and let James Rediron be the *okimaaw*? You can't do that!"

"I don't intend to. I will step aside, I think, in a way that will let me choose the one who follows me." He was breathing heavily. "I think and think who it could be and I keep coming back to Marvin. What about him? Would he lead the people in honesty and wisdom?"

"Marvin?" Old Rabbit Ear's pride swelled. His grandson the chief of the tribe? If that happened, he could go to his grave with joy.

"*Ehe*, Marvin is a man."

"And he values the old ways." Jeremiah's voice shook with emotion. "He would lead our people well, George. He would make a good *okimaaw*!"

"It seems so to me. And I think it is better that we turn the leadership to him now, rather than risk getting a weakling as our chief."

That night Jeremiah crooned a power song to the Thunder spirit and burnt sweet grass and tobacco and promised him two lengths of cloth and a hunting knife for what he had done to help his grandson. The old man wished he still had strength in his legs to go and tell Marvin of the good thing that was going to happen to him. But he didn't. He didn't even have the strength to send his spirit to tell his grandson that George Beardy had decided he was to be the new *okimaaw* of the reserve. He

160

didn't have the strength for a conjuring lodge. But even that didn't matter. Marvin would learn of it soon enough.

The afternoon of Laraviere's funeral the RCMP and a man from the Hudson Bay Company flew in to Birch Lake; the former to investigate the fire and Laraviere's death, the latter to see what could be done about putting up a new building and getting the store back in operation. The two men attended the funeral before seeking out the chief for questioning.

"Who could've done this thing, George?" the Mountie asked quietly.

Beardy shrugged. "Any of us could have done it, I suppose, but I don't know who did." He was glad he had no information to give the officer.

"Post and that black agitator from the States were here, weren't they?"

"*Kawin.*" He shook his head. "Not since the snows have grown old."

"But they were here?"

"Months ago."

"And who did they talk to?"

The chief's eyes narrowed. "Many of us." He gestured widely.

"But who listened?"

Beardy pretended not to know what he meant.

"Who paid attention to his words? Did anyone else besides James Rediron?"

"James is a fool."

"But he did go off to help Post, didn't he?"

"What help would a boy like Rediron be?"

The Mountie tried another line of questioning. "James had come back before the fire, hadn't he?"

George smiled bleakly. "Is it wrong for a man to come back to the reserve? Should we get permission from Indian Affairs for that, too?"

The Mountie swore. "Confound it, man, we've got to find out what happened."

For the first time the chief allowed his own hurt to fleck his

161

eyes. "It was an accident — a terrible accident that took the life of our friend."

The officer continued to question him, but soon gave it up as useless. He had the same results with the others. They were all courteous to him and answered his questions gravely and with respect, but no one seemed to know anything. He didn't even get any information when he picked up a bottle on the table and held it up significantly.

"You wouldn't want me to take you in on a charge of bootlegging, would you?" he asked blandly.

Fear leaped high in the Indian's eyes, but he said, "I tell you, I don't know who set the fire that killed Laraviere. I don't even know if it was set."

"You don't expect me to believe that, do you?"

"It is the truth!" Briefly the hostility was sharp between them.

Though the RCMP sergeant continued to question the people, he was able to learn nothing.

"Did you find out anything, Jack?" the Hudson Bay official asked when they were alone that night.

Sighing, the Mountie slouched into the chair closest to the furnace register in the living room of the company house where Laraviere had lived until his death.

"I found out that the old Frenchman was the best loved man on the reserve — but I already knew that."

"What about his death? Did you get any leads?"

"I didn't expect any from the people. They never tell us anything in a case like this."

"But this is murder."

The Mountie did not agree. "If it were murder, Beardy would know about it; and if he knew such a thing, he would tell us. He's a good chief and a just man."

The officer did not discontinue the investigation until he had visited everyone who could possibly have given him any information. He also searched the remains of the building for some bit of evidence that would burst the steel bands of silence that kept the truth from them. At last, frustrated by the emptiness and futility of the search, the Mountie left. The next day the man from Hudson Bay did the same.

The Hudson Bay Company averted an emergency of major proportions on the reserve by buying a couple of cabooses and setting them, end to end, near the site of the former building. The following week a temporary manager and the first load of supplies were flown into the reserve. The aircraft shuttled back and forth until the improvised store was well stocked again. Even the barrels of gasoline were replaced. They had to be, as gas was the lifeblood of the reserve.

Outwardly all seemed normal in the village. The older men shuffled aimlessly up and down the paths, stopping in one house or another to visit before plodding on. The new manager of the store was nice enough, but it wasn't the same as it had been when Laraviere was there. The Frenchman had enjoyed them, joining in their discussions or sitting silently in perfect ease with them for an hour or more, the way they did themselves.

Then, too, the cabooses were stacked with groceries and clothes and ammunition. There wasn't room for the men to gather about the stove. So they went to the store for the things they needed, paused wistfully at the counter to say a few words to the new manager, and left. Something was gone from their lives.

The women were as busy as usual, cutting wood and carrying water and trying to stretch their meagre supply of macaroni and flour and tea to provide another meal. The children played as happily as ever in the village.

A visitor would have been unaware of it, but the reserve was wrapped in gloom. The fire that had destroyed the store and taken Laraviere's life had left only the twisting, acrid smoke to remind them of what might have been.

The quick sureness was gone from the step of the young men and resignation and hopelessness dimmed their eyes. The RCMP had been back twice, still firing questions, still looking for the crack that would allow them to pry out the truth.

After a few days Rediron came slinking back, disappointment lingering in his solemn face.

"Where've you been?" Stanley wanted to know.

"I — I thought it was best if I — I wasn't around for a little while."

"The Mounties've been asking about you."

James winced. "What difference does that make? I ain't scared of them."

"The old men are hard against you. They say you are afraid and that a coward isn't fit to be our chief."

James tried to act unconcerned. "They'll change their minds when Post and Otis talk to them."

"That's another thing. They aren't going to let either the white man or the American back on the reserve."

"And," Vetel added, "there is talk that the council is going to name Marvin Lacendre as the new chief!"

23

STILL SMARTING FROM her husband's scorn, Tina Norris got the front bedroom ready for the injured man Bruce would soon be bringing home. Resentment flared in her usually mild eyes. It was only going to be for one night, she could tell him that. She started to put an extra blanket on the bed but changed her mind and stripped off the sheets first. She didn't care what Bruce said; she wasn't going to have an — an Indian sleeping on her best sheets.

She didn't know why he insisted on bringing one of *those* people into the house when he *knew* how she felt about them. There were plenty of Indian homes in the settlement where the stranger would be welcome. Bruce could give him an injection of morphine to ease the pain and let him stay there until the QSO brought the air ambulance to take him out.

She was spreading the blankets on the bed when her lanky husband came home with two Indian fellows carrying Marvin on an improvised stretcher.

"Help us get him into bed, Tina," he said evenly.

The simple request infuriated her.

"He's in shock and running quite a fever. Better get another blanket, too."

"Yes, sir!" She did as she was told, but with her temper smoldering. If she was going to be treated like a nurse's aid, she'd act like one.

But Bruce didn't seem to notice. He took Marvin's temperature and pulse once more and gave him an injection.

Tina was waiting when he came out of the bedroom and pulled the door shut behind him.

"How is he?"

"He's determined not to go to the hospital, for some reason. I finally told him that we'd take care of him here."

She jerked erect. "You what?"

"I can take care of him all right. His burns are superficial and the fracture is simple. A good first-aid man could take care of him."

"That isn't exactly what I was referring to," she retorted icily.

"What's gotten into you, Tina? We've been praying for these people since we came here. Now we've got a chance to have one of them in our home for awhile. We both ought to thank God for the opportunity."

Tina stared at him. It was useless to argue with him, she realized.

Bruce Norris radioed for setting plaster and surgical gauze, and when it came he set Marvin's leg and put the cast on it from the bottom of his foot to a point several inches above the knee.

"Now I can go back to the reserve," Marvin said.

"I'm sorry, but you're not going to be able to leave for a week or two."

Marvin lay back and closed his eyes, luxuriating in the softness of the clean white bed that had kept him awake at first.

He was glad the field officer had stuck the needle into his hip before setting the broken bone. The pain had been so bad that it was all he could do to keep from crying out his agony. He didn't know whether the medicine had stolen the pain or not, but he was free from it. He closed his eyes and drew in a long breath. He was lying motionless, half asleep, when a sweet young voice drifted into his consciousness.

"Hello."

He struggled to open one eye.

"Good afternoon, Marvin."

166

Her warm smile tugged the corners of his lips upward. He judged her to be four or five years old, a miniature replica of her mother. She had come to the door on other occasions and two or three times had slipped in to talk to him, but only for a moment.

Nick, who was younger, popped in and out at all hours, but Juli had the shyness of a fawn and the same tenderness in her eyes that her father had.

"Mommy said I could come in and see you this afternoon."

That was strange, Marvin reasoned. He had sensed Tina's dislike and fear of him from the first night they brought him to the house.

"I came to tell you a story," Juli explained. She pulled a chair close beside the bed. "Do you like stories?"

"*Ehe.*" He meant to use English but Cree slipped out.

Her laughter tinkled. "That's a funny way to talk."

He heard the footsteps outside his room and looked up in time to see Tina watching, disapproval in her eyes.

"Maybe you'd better come out now, Juli. Mr. Lacendre is tired."

"But I haven't told him my story yet," she protested.

Reluctantly Tina gave permission to stay.

Marvin was only half listening when she began, her voice hushed with the horror of the tale she was about to share with him.

"Way — way out in the bush where there wasn't any village and no radios or float planes or kicker boats there was this great 'normous wolf, see?"

The question in her voice jerked his attention back to her. "*Ehe.* Yes," he corrected quickly.

"This great, 'normous wolf had eyes as — as big as clam shells and the biggest, hugest, awfullest teeth you ever saw. And smoke came out of his mouth whenever he breathed, and he roamed around the muskeg and caught and ate an Indian man for breakfast every day. He even had one for dinner if he could find an extra one."

"Juli!" Tina broke in.

"It isn't a bad story, mommy," she said. "I'm not going to have him eat Marvin up. I'm just going to have him get terrible scared."

"Well, you'd better stop this and scoot out of here or none of us will be able to sleep tonight."

When the girl was gone, Tina came over to Marvin's bed. It was difficult for her to understand why, but she was beginning to like this dark-skinned young man who had been a guest in their home for a week.

"Is there anything I can get for you?"

"My rifle." His face was somber.

She gasped. "Your — your rifle?"

"I want to be ready when that wolf of Juli's comes around looking for his breakfast."

For the first time since he had been in her home, Tina Norris laughed.

That evening she asked him to come out to the dining room to eat with them. He came, hobbling awkwardly on the crutches the field officer had gotten for him.

"We can thank God the break in your leg was no worse than it was," Bruce said.

Marvin had heard his grandfather speak of the spirits that way, but he had never known any white man to have such reverence for his God that he talked of Him in such a manner. A little later he was even more bewildered. The field officer got a Bible and read from it.

That night Marvin thought about Jesus Christ who was able to make a blind man see and a lame man walk. He wondered if that meant God could heal his leg as though it had never been broken. A religion like that would be a good thing, he decided. A guy wouldn't have to be afraid of anything.

He hoped Norris would read more about this God the following night so he could understand more about Him. It was better hearing it from his lips than from the woman, Miss Bannister. She had only been a woman. She wouldn't have anything that could be of interest to a man as far as religion was concerned.

The field officer did read more from the Bible the next night and the next and the next, but the parts he read were even more

168

bewildering. He read that man was a sinner; that he didn't want to do good things but only bad. And God wouldn't have a man like that in heaven.

Marvin saw, then, that it wouldn't do any good for him to try to get a God like that to help him. He would bust anyone else in the mouth for saying it, but he knew the sort of man he was. It was wrong to drink and gamble and chase women the way he did. A terrible feeling of guilt swept over him.

Bruce read about hell, too. Marvin had heard guys joke about it, saying they wanted to go there so they would be with their friends, but it hadn't seemed like a real place to him then.

He listened to the Bible reading and Bruce Norris's calm explanations. "But Jesus can give you a new life. He can take away your sin and make your heart as though you had never done anything bad. He can make you clean in God's sight."

This was something Marvin had to ponder, exploring each facet and making sure it was what he wanted for his life. His grandfather would say this was the white man's religion and wasn't for the Indian, but Norris talked as though that didn't make any difference.

Not that his new white friend tried to pressure him. If he had, Marvin would not have been able to refuse whether he understood what it meant to have a personal relationship with God or not. But Bruce talked quietly with him, giving him time to consider the matter.

"Think it over for a few days, Marvin."

Marvin considered it until the time approached that he should leave, but without resolve. He was still thinking about it, even as he pressured the field officer to let him go back to the reserve for awhile.

That night almost as soon as Marvin closed his eyes, the Robin appeared to him. She didn't speak. She didn't have to. Anger clouded her beautiful face and twisted the corners of her mouth. Terrified, he awakened quickly. This was a sign! An omen!

He hadn't even started to plan for the sun dance and now he was listening to the white man read to him about God. It was small wonder the Robin was angry!

He cried aloud!

Bruce heard him and rushed to his room. "Are you all right?"

He sat up, shaken. He couldn't tell the white man what was wrong. Norris wouldn't understand. But he would have the sun dance. As soon as he got home he would begin to plan for it.

He dared not sleep the rest of the night. Only once or twice did he even permit his eyes to close. He wasn't going to have the Robin appear to him again if he could help it. But when he got up the next morning she was there, hopping about the lawn. He shuddered when he saw her and turned quickly away from the window.

As he stood there a new thought sneaked through the cracks of his mind. He didn't know why it hadn't come before, but what could the Robin do for him or to him for that matter? He had already decided to give the sun dance and was beginning to make preliminary plans for it at the time of the fire and Laraviere's death. His spirit-helper was supposed to be so happy that she would do many good things for him. But she hadn't even been able to help him get Laraviere out of the burning store building alive, and she hadn't kept him from getting hurt. What good was a spirit-helper like that? It made him wonder whether his spirit-helper was worth the effort and time to have the sun dance.

Maybe Norris was right, he reasoned. Maybe this Jesus Christ he read about in the Bible was a better God to put his trust in than the spirits his own people used to worship. Grimly he tried to push that thought aside, but it persisted in coming back, nagging at him relentlessly.

The next day Marvin talked with Norris once more about going back to Birch Lake. When the field officer saw that Marvin honestly wanted to leave, he said it would be all right for him to go.

"But I'd like to have you come back in six weeks to have the cast taken off your leg. Okay?"

"I'll be back in six weeks," Marvin promised.

Tina came to Marvin before he left. "I'm sorry for the way I treated you when you first came," she told him.

His gaze was questioning. There was no knowing what these white people meant by the things they said. Of course he had known she didn't like it that her husband had brought him home. He had sensed it in little ways he could not have explained, but why would she apologize to him?

"You have taught me much about your people," Tina continued. "I want to thank you for it."

Marvin hesitantly shook the hand she offered.

She watched while Marvin went down to the lake and got into the aircraft that would drop him off at the reserve. It had not been easy having the young Indian stay in their home and taking care of him. It had not been easy for her to offer him her hand in spite of the fact that she had grown to like him. All the old resentments, prejudices, and fears had churned within her as she made the simple gesture.

But a chink had been forced in her wall of hatred against the Indians. She saw Marvin as an individual, the same as herself.

Bruce came up beside her and squeezed her shoulder affectionately. Briefly she sagged against him.

24

Jeremiah was at the dock to meet Marvin when he got off the plane.

"I would talk to you," the old man told him.

He was searching the crowd for Aldina. "Not now."

"George Beardy and the council asked me to come down and see you." His trembling old voice cracked. "Come to the house." His grandfather was not requesting the visit; he was demanding it.

Marvin supposed his grandfather would be alone in the cabin when he got there some minutes later, after a vain effort to find Aldina, but the chief and his council were there. He spoke to them and sat down near the door. Custom dictated a time for small talk, the ritualistic visiting that was the prelude to important meetings among the Cree.

George Beardy inquired about his burns and his leg and expressed the gratitude of the tribal leaders for what he had done.

"Others brought shame and dishonor to our people, but you were a shining candle in the night. Because of you, we are able to hold our heads high once more."

Marvin spoke modestly. "Thank you."

His humbleness was noted by the older men who murmured their approval.

"We want to talk with you about this Rediron."

"*Ehe?*" Marvin straightened at the mention of his rival's name.

"He's been talking to the young men since the RCMP stopped

172

coming around. Like a whiskey jack — talk-talk-talk, making bears of shadows."

"And what does he say?"

"That he should be the chief."

Marvin knew James had talked that way, but he never thought that such talk was strong enough to make the council take note of it.

"Do the people listen?"

"Kawin. The taste of what he did in stirring up the young men is gall in the mouths of the men, but people forget, and if he keeps talking enough, they may decide that what he says is true."

George Beardy nodded. "That is why we have come to you. We have plans for you, Marvin."

"Ehe," Jeremiah broke in. "You are still going to have the sun dance for the Robin, aren't you?"

"That is my plan." Marvin spoke indifferently, as though it didn't matter whether he did or not.

"After the sun dance you will have all the men behind you. Then we will announce that you are going to be the chief in my place."

Marvin's lower jaw slacked in sudden awe. "Me?" he echoed. "The *okimaaw?"*

"Ehe," Jeremiah's voice was triumphant. "It is the decision of George and all the council. We want you to be the chief."

"That will stop James," George Beardy concluded. "We will act before he has time to gain support."

Marvin was stunned. He had dreamed often of being a leader in the village, of being able to help his people, but it had been only a dream, a wistful longing that scarcely had substance enough to label. Now they had spelled it out. The wiser, more concerned leaders of the village were looking to him to guide the tribe. It was more than he could hope for.

"You go now," Jeremiah said, touching his arm proudly. "We have much to talk about here that doesn't concern you yet. We will work on plans for the sun dance after you have had time to rest.

Aldina wasn't at his cabin when he hobbled up to it on his

crutches. It didn't look as though she had been there for some time. Bread on the table was as hard as a chunk of jerky and the smell of spoiled fish pinched at his nostrils.

She came home before the end of the week, her gait unsteady and her eyes dull. It brought pain to his heart to see her that way, even when he was drinking too. But he did not protest. With her it would do no good. She had a will of her own.

Sitting on the bed beside her some time later, he told her about the sun dance he was going to give for the Robin. She thought she liked that, especially when she learned that there was talk that George Beardy might step down as chief and turn the job over to him.

"You?" Her eyes brightened. "James says that he is going to be the *okimaaw*."

"Talk to George," he told her proudly. "It is the truth I'm telling you."

She nodded her acceptance of what he was saying. She did not laugh, nor did she disbelieve him. He had never told her anything that wasn't true.

He didn't care much about the sun dance itself, except for what it would do to make him important among the people, but he set to work carefully, planning it step by step. The sun dance would have to be held at the time of the new moon in June. It was a mid-summer ceremony when the world was green and the winds soft and caressing and the sun reigned in all its glory.

Marvin didn't know why, but thoughts of the God Bruce Norris had read about from the Bible rushed back, and the stories of Jesus Christ flooded his mind. Was he wise in planning a sun dance for a spirit who hadn't even been able to keep him from getting hurt and who allowed his best friend to die? Was it good to take part in such a ceremony when Christ wanted to clean away the sin and give him a new life.

He was so troubled that evening that he got out the testament Norris had given him and tried to read it, but the words only jumbled in his mind.

But the sun dance was not only for the Robin, he reasoned. Even though she hadn't been able to help him much, think of what the religious observance was going to do for him. It would make him chief! The thought was staggering.

Word that he was going to have the sun dance spread rapidly throughout the reserve. Some of the younger ones laughed when they heard it, but he didn't care about that.

Excitement gripped the people in the days that followed. One of Marvin's friends shot a fat bull moose and Aldina dressed it and dried the meat. The nets had good catches of pickerel and jacks, and one fisherman after another brought smoked fish to him to help feed the guests who would be flocking in from everywhere.

"Here is something for the people to eat at the sun dance, cousin," they would say respectfully.

Marvin was pleased with the plans that were being made and so was his grandfather.

"I've already taught you the power songs," Jeremiah told him. "I will take care of everything else to see that all is in order."

Marvin was glad for his grandfather's assistance. No one else on the reserve had ever held a sundance. No one else knew about the selection of the devoted tree to become the sun pole or about finding the buffalo skull and painting and ornamenting it. They didn't know about the buffalo dance which was held first in the sun dance lodge before the sun-gazing dance.

Who else knew about the goose-bone whistles and the ritual of smoking the pipes? Who, indeed, among all the old ones even knew about all the ceremonies and rituals that went into a proper sun dance?

Marvin was so busy with the coming ceremony he didn't even remember he was supposed to go back to Deauval to have his cast removed until he noticed the date circled on his calendar.

"You mean you are leaving now?" Aldina demanded, her scowl indicating her disapproval. "It is only a week until the sun dance."

He did not answer her directly. That, he had long since learned, could only lead to quarreling.

"Did you finish the caribou moccasins I asked you to make me for the little girl?"

"*Ehe.*" She got them. "A new girl friend?" Her eyes were bright with anger.

"With a foot so small?" he laughed.

"Or maybe it's her mother you're trying to be friends with."

Marvin could have slapped her.

James Rediron knew Marvin had gone to Deauval to have the cast removed from his leg. He had watched him leave, his resentment smoldering. Aldina would be alone for three or four days, time enough for him to renew his friendship with her without risking a collision with Marvin.

He had a bottle of whiskey and two boxes of cigarettes hidden in the folds of the jacket he was carrying. He had been saving them for such an occasion, but he would have to hurry, he told himself, or someone else would beat him to her.

Marvin had been thinking a lot about Bruce and Tina Norris and their Bible readings and the talks they had with him. The things they said were both bitter and sweet. They kept him from sleeping at night and put barbs on his thoughts to torture his days.

He wasn't going to allow them to talk to him of Jesus this time, he decided. He would get there, have the cast taken off, and leave as soon as possible.

But when he got to Deauval, Bruce was gone and wouldn't be back until later in the afternoon.

"You should plan on spending the night here," Tina told him. "I know Bruce would want that."

"No," he answered crisply. "I will stay with my cousin." He referred to an Indian he had met on his previous visit. Had the invitation to stay the night come from the field officer he would have accepted it, but a man didn't like to have his wife speak for him. It was the place of the man to ask.

Shortly before supper that night Bruce came down to the house where he was staying and insisted he come up with them. "Juli and Tina both want to see you."

Marvin had been surprised at the friendliness in the white woman's voice when he saw her earlier in the day. It was different than Aldina's friendliness with men. That would have shamed them all. A man does not rob the traps of a friend or carry off his brother's moose. Tina was friendly in the way a sister would have been friendly.

"After dinner I'll take the cast off and have a look at your leg."

Only it was not to be, at least not as quickly as Bruce planned. When they finished eating and Juli had been sent to bed, still clutching her new white moccasins, Bruce and Tina talked with Marvin once more of Jesus Christ. They talked again of sin and the One called Jesus who could give a man a clean heart and a new life.

It mattered not what he had done or how he had lived, they told him. If he wanted Jesus to take him, He would, and his life would become as fresh and pure as new snow or the water in a river far from any village.

At last it was more than he could bear. "I want to walk the Jesus way!"

But Bruce and his wife did not pray with him immediately.

"It's not going to be easy for you to live a Christian life among your own people. You'll be misunderstood and ridiculed. You may even be hated by some of your old friends."

The brawny Indian's hands were working nervously. What Norris said was true. It would not be easy for him to walk the Jesus way. The old ones would be furious because he had forsaken the old ways. The young ones would laugh him to scorn. And there was Aldina. Always there was Aldina.

But at that moment none of those things made a difference to him. The Jesus way was the way a man should go. It would put his feet on the path they should follow.

"*Ehe,*" he murmured in assent. "It will be hard, maybe. But a man does not shrink from that which is good just because it may be hard."

That was the happiest night Marvin ever spent. The field officer read to him from the Bible, explaining what it meant, and he snatched at every word.

"You are going back tomorrow?" Bruce finally asked.

The Indian hesitated. "I will have to see," he hedged.

Some time that evening, long after the cast had been removed and the leg pronounced strong and well, Marvin knelt with the

Norrises, confessed his sin, and asked God to give him a new life in Christ.

He planned on going home immediately, but that was put aside, unremembered. For the next three or four days he remained at Deauval, spending as much time as possible with the field officer and his wife, learning about the Word of God and what it had to say to him. As he listened and asked questions, it was as though his burdens were pushed aside and for the first time in his life he was free. Forgotten was Aldina, his grandfather, the sun dance — everything except this wonderful new life that had come to him.

It was not until he saw a robin hopping across the lawn that he remembered. He winced as thought of the sun dance came rushing back. The people would already have gathered at Birch Lake and would be looking for him. He glanced around uneasily, a great ache building within him.

"I have to get back," he mumbled. "I have to leave in the morning."

The next day while the hush of the new dawn was still on the village, Marvin filled the borrowed kicker with gas and nosed into the river. He had to get back to the reserve as soon as possible. Already many of the preparations had been completed.

25

FOR THE MOMENT James Rediron forgot Aldina, although she still clung to him, begging for his lips. He sprawled at the table, jealous fingers encircling their last bottle of cheap whiskey. Through the half-open door of Marvin's cabin he could look across the lake and down the silver slot that was the river.

It was not a pleasant stream, that one. It squirmed across forest-hidden muskeg and outcroppings of the precambrian shield, widened into lakes, and narrowed to tumble noisily over great, canoe-shattering boulders that crouched out of sight in the frenzied current. It was a wild, unsporting river as unstable and explosive as the black-haired temptress beside him who shared her bed with him while her man was gone. A river given to grabbing the unsuspecting boat and dashing it to destruction.

Only a man who knew no fear would dare to use such a river as a road from Deauval. Only a man like Marvin Lacendre. He would come bucking upstream, defying rocks and churning water, laughter on his lips and his powerful outboard kicker screaming. To Marvin, the river was a challenge, an enemy to be faced and conquered.

James cursed silently. He wished that broad-shouldered moose of a Marvin would get drunk in Deauval and stay stiff for a week. He wished he would misjudge the river and smash his boat; anything to keep him from getting back to the reserve before time for the sun dance.

James knew well enough what the old men of the reserve thought of him since the fire that had caused Laraviere's death.

He had felt bad about that himself, and was only glad they hadn't told the RCMP about his part in stirring up trouble. He knew, too, about the plan Beardy had for Marvin after the sun dance. He had wormed the information out of Aldina during a drunken argument.

He had to do something about it now or all was lost! And there was nothing he could do if Marvin came back. He wished he was big enough to lie in wait for him on the narrow river and put a stop to his return! But he had tangled with Marvin once. He didn't want to risk that again.

He had plans for that sun dance and Marvin's reputation among the people — if only he stayed away for another day!

James Rediron's fingers contracted, tightening convulsively about the bottle. He was drunk, but not too drunk to plan.

Aldina pulled herself erect, drunken fingers fumbling to fasten the top button on her blouse.

"I don't have to stay here with you," she reminded him.

The swarthy Cree's fingers relaxed about the bottle. He had done himself a lot of harm when violence exploded and the old Frenchman was killed, but the people could be made to forget that. Then he could be their leader and Post would be glad to have his help again.

"If you're just goin' to sit there," she pouted, "I'm goin' to have another drink."

She reached uncertainly for the bottle, her hand finding it and closing about the neck. He wrenched it from her angrily, spilling a few drops on the rough table.

"Look what you made me do!" He clenched his fist and gestured threateningly in her direction.

"You wouldn't dare! Marvin would tear you apart!"

He flinched at the mention of his rival's name. The movement was so slight he was scarcely aware of it himself, but she had seen it.

"The big brave James Rediron!"

His eyes blazed and his fist knotted. "Shut your big mouth!"

She said no more to him, but a thin, provocative smile rested lightly on her lips. Trying to close out her obvious amusement at his fear, he tilted the bottle high and the molten liquid cut a furrow in his throat.

Her mood changed abrubtly. Her eyes softened and she moved closer to him, caressing his cheek with her hand. He allowed her to take the whiskey and finish the bottle in one long draught.

"The people are comin' from everywhere for Marvin's sun dance," she said, pride swelling in her voice.

"Marvin's sun dance!" he exploded. "Have you heard the people talkin' the last couple of days?"

"About what?"

"About me!"

"You?" Her laughter whipped him raw. "I've heard what they've been sayin' about you since the RCMP came in and you sneaked off into the bush to hide like a frightened wood mouse. I know what they're calling you!"

"You wait! Just you wait!"

"You, the chief?" She laughed again until the tears stained her cheeks.

"You'll see. I'll be the *okimaaw* and have plenty of money. You'll wish, then, that you'd stayed with me."

Her eyes mocked him.

"I can always come back to you," she reminded him scornfully. "Any time I want."

Jeremiah Rabbit Ear hobbled along the village path, his tottering legs propped by a willow staff that sagged under the weight he rested on it. Slowly he approached the huge circle of tents that surrounded the place of the sun dance, his moccasins scuffing the hard ground.

The bony old man, face crinkled as pine bark, had always been small of stature, even for a Cree. Advancing years had melted his flesh away and arthritis folded him half double and shrank his gaunt frame. Now he was scarcely bigger than a tamarack sapling among the jack pine.

He had long since resigned himself to the fact that he would die almost as a man without a people. But now there was to be another sun dance on the reserve and people would be coming from everywhere to take part in it. The thought was enough to warm him inwardly and quicken his pulse. His own grandson was the one who was bringing this to pass. And, as if that was not enough to complete his joy, Marvin was to be the new chief. George Beardy and the council had chosen him out of all the young men in the village.

"Jeremiah!"

He stopped at the sound of his name. That was George again.

"The council would see you," the chief said.

He straightened testily. "Don't they know I'm busy?"

"*Ehe,*" Beardy murmured. "But they would speak to you."

The load of the sun dance weighed heavily on his bent shoulders. He was the only one on the reserve who knew all about the ceremony. Who else had saved the buffalo skull from the old days? Who else would know how to make the thunderbird's nest for the top of the sacred pole?

"Marvin is not back from Deauval yet," the chief reminded him.

"He will be," Jeremiah snapped, eyes narrowing.

"It is James who is making trouble for the council," the chief explained. "He tells everyone that Marvin will not be back and says that he should be given permission to give the sun dance."

Jeremiah spat his contempt. "Tell them that Marvin will be back in time."

"They want to hear it from your lips."

"I will talk to them." He pounded the ground savagely with his willow cane. "I'll talk to them!"

Straightening his powerful frame, Marvin shook off the cold spray that spumed up from the bow of his sturdy, borrowed boat and drenched him. The early morning sun gleamed on the rapids ahead, catching the white plumes of dancing water with dazzling fingers that hurt his eyes.

Anticipation split the gloom in his broad face as he approached the familiar stretch of rough water. This was a bad spot. He had almost lost both his boat and his life the first time he tried it.

He could have gone around the way everyone else did, but the thought had never occurred to him. A simple, direct individual, he faced what came. Even now that he had shifted his allegiance from his spirit-helper to Jesus Christ, he made no attempt to avoid the Robin or her domain.

Squinting, he approached the rapids without hesitation, chose his course, and drove for it. He slammed around a huge boulder, the ugly sentinel at the foot of the rapids, and fought his way up the narrow trough with rocks crowding in on either side, so close the inexperienced would swear there was no space for a boat to skin through. But twist through he did, sweeping wide on the next bed to avoid the certain disaster he knew lay hidden in the treacherous, foaming water close to the bank.

Every blow shot pains from his ankle to his hip. Grimly he fought against the shuddering, throbbing pain, thrusting it aside with a rough hand. He was used to ignoring pain and discomfort.

The trip had changed him. How it had changed him. He had wanted to stay in Deauval even longer than he had, hearing those things the Norrises read to him out of the Holy Book and listening to them pray.

Jesus Christ was strong — strong enough to give him a new life. He was stronger than the Robin and his grandfather's spirit-helper, the Thunder. He was more powerful than all the spirits. He had taken the longing to do bad things out of Marvin's heart and made him want to do good.

It would have been easy for him to have remained in Deauval another week or two. But he couldn't do that. He had told his grandfather and Beardy and the council that he would be back in time for the ceremony. He had to keep his word.

He was thinking about Aldina as he nosed out of the river and angled across one corner of the big lake. As soon as he was close enough, he began to search the hillside eagerly for her. There were strange tents ringing the clearing, jammed one against the other. Women were crouched about a dozen or more small fires, stirring the contents of huge iron kettles and, now and then, looking up at the kids who were everywhere. The men were clustered on the steps of the Bay store or sprawled on the grass beside the fish buyer's new ice house. The younger ones had gone some distance from the others and were leaning against the brilliantly painted handmade boats that were pulled out of the water on wooden rollers. And wherever the men were gathered, they were talking endlessly.

Marvin searched intently for Aldina, but her distinctive bright dress was not in sight; nor was there any smoke twisting upward from his chimney against the deep green of the forest.

He recognized two figures on the government dock before he was close enough to distinguish anyone else; his grandfather and Beardy.

"I am glad you're back," Jeremiah said moments later. "There are those who have been afraid you wouldn't get here in time."

"It was not me who doubted it," Beardy retorted testily. "How many times do I have to tell you that?"

Dimly Marvin heard what they were saying as they talked about the portions of the ceremony that they had already held, the cutting of the devotion tree, the making of the altar, and the giving of banners to those who had taken the vow of thirst and hunger until the sun went down the following day. He was looking over their heads, his gaze searching the slope for Aldina.

As soon as he could, he hobbled up the steep slope and along the narrow, twisting path to his cabin. With each painful step his exhaustion increased and once or twice he stopped to rest.

His gaze swept the little cabin. Aldina had been staying there since he went away, and from the looks of things, she had not been alone. Wearily he dropped to the bunk, pulled the moccasin from his swollen foot, and lay down. He was still asleep the following morning when there was a knock at the door.

He stirred restlessly and shook himself awake.

"Rabbit Ear says the people wait. It is time for you to come," a youthful voice told him.

He lay still for a moment gazing up at the rough ceiling. The boy who had brought the message must have scampered away.

Having the sun dance would help him gain the support of the people so Beardy could make him the new chief, but another question came back to plague him. The question that had been hammering at him since he had made his decision to follow the

184

way of Jesus Christ. What would He think if this new son of His would hold a sun dance for the spirit-helper of his old life?

Marvin had tried to talk to God about it, explaining about the people who had come from faraway and that he could not disappoint them, but he was so inexperienced in talking to Jesus that he didn't know whether he had been heard or not.

"I will not mean it when I sing the sacred songs," he assured his Savior. "And I won't mean it when I say prayers to the Robin. You and I will know that they are only words. My heart will be locked against them."

The others, however, would not know that he did not speak from his heart. And that was the trouble. They would think he still worshiped the Robin, and if he would ever talk with Aldina or his grandfather about this Jesus Christ who could give them new lives, they would wonder at his having the sun dance.

Slowly he swung his feet over the edge of the bunk and sat up, his great shoulders sagging. After a moment he stooped mechanically and picked up the moccasin. For a time he clutched it between rough fingers. He still had not moved to put it on when the door creaked open.

Aldina came in, silhouetted for an instant in the doorway.

"*Waaci*, Marvin." Her voice was husky and sensuous.

"You finally came back."

"Don't be that way." She minced across the floor and stooped to kiss him, conscious of the allure her lithe, thinly-clad body had for him. He stood and pulled her young figure close.

"I missed you."

"It is time to start," she murmured. "The people are waiting."

"I know." He released her and stepped back, still holding the moccasin in his hand.

He studied her features closely. It was hard for him to believe she was the same woman he had taken from James half a year ago. It was harder yet to believe that his very being burned at the sight of her. Yet the feeling was still there.

Aldina leaned close to him. "We've got to go," she repeated.

"*Ehe*." With that he picked up the beaded moosehide jacket she had made for him and slipped it on.

26

Marvin bent through the door and followed Aldina, but he stopped on the trail for so long that she turned and rushed back, annoyance smoldering in her eyes.

"Hurry!"

He followed her silently until they reached the crowd. Everyone was staring at him. For some reason he did not quite understand, he cringed under the admiring gaze of the people.

Near the lodge, he stopped.

His grandfather had constructed it according to the time-honored plan. It was a large structure built on poles anchored in the ground. The sides were thatched with poplar branches, but the roof, save for the poles, was open so the dancers could see the sun. The sacred pole was in the center with the thunderbird's nest at its top. A thunderbird had been painted two or three feet below the nest and lengths of cloth were suspended from the sacred pole or piled, one over the other, around it.

Jeremiah had done his work well. The altar had even been dug and the objects of veneration placed in their prescribed places.

Everyone was waiting for a shrill blast or two on the goose-bone whistles, a proper smoking of the pipes, the roll of drums, and Marvin's power song so the dancing could begin. Some people, in anticipation of that happy moment, were ready to file into the enclosure and take their places — the women in the southeast portion and the men along the western arc. The proper thing had to be done in a proper manner, but Jeremiah knew all of these things. And so the sun dance had been correctly planned and they waited now for the starting of the climaxing ceremony.

The crowd was waiting in silence for Marvin to do his part in opening the dance. It was a simple thing, a short chant extolling the virtues of the Robin and how powerful he had become now that she was his spirit. After the first few lines of his chant, the most important work he had to do would be over. Others could carry on from there.

But would his part really be over when the sun dance was begun? Could he do this thing now that he walked the Jesus way? Slowly his gaze drifted from one upturned face to another. Admiration glinted in Aldina's eyes. She enjoyed the feeling of power, the honor of being the lover of one so important in the village.

"I called this sun dance," he began, "in honor of the Robin because she had done something very special for me."

Jeremiah frowned his surprise and disapproval. What was wrong with his grandson? Didn't he know this was to be in his power chant?

Aldina lowered her head and a proud flush spread across her brown cheeks.

"But when I went to Deauval after I got hurt, I heard for the first time about the Lord Jesus Christ who saves from sin." He paused, held by the hush of the moment.

"That's white man's religion!" Jeremiah muttered in horror.

Marvin drew himself even taller. "Jesus is not only for the white man. He is also for the Cree."

He stopped once more. He could still end this talk of Christ. The people would forget what he had said if he went into the lodge and began his power chant. He could still be the chief and be able to help his people. But he could not deny his Lord.

"I now walk the Jesus way. I no longer follow the spirits."

The crimson leaked from Aldina's face, leaving her cheeks ashen and rage gleaming in her eyes.

"I know great joy and peace since I follow Jesus."

He would have said more, but Aldina, who was the first in

the crowd to move, shuffled closer to him, stopping a pace or so away.

"Hah!" With that she came forward and slapped him savagely on the cheek with all the strength of her supple young body. The print of her hand showed white against the bronze of his skin. He recoiled at the force of the blow, staggering backwards. Then still moving with maddening deliberation, she turned and walked across the open space to where James Rediron was standing. Brazenly she put her arms about his neck and kissed him passionately.

Rediron froze, arms at his side. Marvin would kill him for this! There was no way he could escape. In an instant those powerful, bearlike arms would grab him and he would be finished.

"I – I – " He pulled away from her.

Aldina read his fear and stepped back, humiliation feeding the anger that raged within.

"You coward!" Her voice was shrill. "You miserable coward!" She slapped him and turned away as laughter tittered across the crowd.

James stared helplessly after her. It was all over for him. The death of Laraviere had been a severe blow. This would finish him in the eyes of his most faithful supporters. He was branded a coward before all the people of the reserve and most of those from the neighboring settlements. Word of this would spread through the north. No one would ever listen to him again.

The laughter rang in his ears as he turned and slunk away.

Marvin, watching Rediron's sagging shoulders, was surprised at his own lack of joy at seeing his rival crushed and beaten. He hadn't noticed, either, that his grandfather had regained his composure and was approaching him. Crooked fingers touched his arm and he pivoted.

"I'm sorry, grandfather."

Rage exploded across the old man's seamed features. "You're no grandson of mine!" He spat in Marvin's face.

George Beardy gasped and moved forward involuntarily, expecting Marvin to smash Jeremiah in the mouth. Marvin's fist clenched and trembled to be unleashed. Then he relaxed, wiped the spit from his face, and spoke quietly.

"I'm sorry, grandfather," he repeated.

At that moment Beardy spoke. "There has been enough of this! We have all come for a sun dance and the sun dance will go on."

"No! The pledger is gone!" Jeremiah cried.

"Jeremiah Rabbit Ear will be the pledger. He has done all of the planning, all of the building. It is only fitting that the dance be his."

Beardy grasped Jeremiah's arm and gently guided him into the lodge. A moment later the old man's voice was raised in the quavering notes of the power song. The drums took up the beat and the sun dance began.

Marvin stared at the people who had turned away from him as scornfully as though the color of his skin had just been discovered as white. He did not move, however, until the musicians joined on their goose-bone whistles, swaying to the beat. This was no place for him now. His day of influence on the Birch Lake reserve was ended. He turned and walked toward his cabin.

He didn't know whether he would stay in the village any longer or not. There would be no danger for him if he should, although that would not have affected him one way or the other. He had never known fear of another man, and it wouldn't come now.

As far as the people were concerned, it would be as though he had gone away. They would look past him when they met him on the paths and would pretend he didn't join their little groups on the dock or in the Bay. He would be a stranger in his own land and among his own people.

The chances were that his grandfather would never speak to him again. He felt badly about that for he loved the old man.

And Aldina was gone forever. That was what her eyes had told him the instant before she attempted to shame him with her open hand against his cheek. He could still feel the burning of the blow.

He would never be the chief of the reserve, but neither would

James. Branded a coward, Rediron would never be able to win a following again.

And Post was finished in the area as well. James Rediron's cowardice would also brand Post and Ray Otis, although they had nothing to do with it. And word would spread to the other reserves. Already there were deep misgivings about the two because of Laraviere, and this would end their influence. Marvin was glad of that.

As he shuffled along the deserted path, he became aware of a new longing that burned within his heart. He had to help his people. Ever since Post first talked to him, he had been stirred about the injustices and wanted to do what he could to right them.

It was true that their treaty rights had been violated, that welfare robbed them of self-respect and kept them firmly gripped in poverty. They needed help, but it had to come by being given opportunities to work and advance and take care of themselves and their families. The stigma against being Indian had to be replaced by pride.

To accomplish those things, the Indians must get together and speak one voice in dignity. Regina, Winnipeg, and Ottawa would all have to be approached.

Work would have to be done among his people, too, making them see their own value as individuals. The hanging head and the cowering manner had to go. They had to be taught to walk as free men.

And more than that, his people had to hear the good news of the gospel of Christ. He didn't know much about the Bible, but he had read in one place where Jesus said that even the hairs of a man's head were numbered. The way he saw it, that meant God really cared about each person. He must have, or He wouldn't have sent His Son to die on the Cross so everyone who wanted to could be saved.

It was things like that which brought a man's head up and put confidence into his step. He would talk to his people about what Jesus Christ had done for him and what He could do for them. He would make them see that only Christ could make them truly free.

He paused and for a moment turned back to the sun dance lodge. But how could he talk to the people? He, more than anyone else, felt their anger.

It was like Norris had said: there would be times when it wouldn't be easy to walk the Jesus way. And this must be one of those times. And there would be times when there would be hard choices for a man to make.

The frown lines about his face softened. What had Bruce and Tina said about God answering prayer? He had softened his heart when it was set as stone against Him. He could soften the hearts of the people as well.

He would stay. And he would pray, trusting God to melt away the anger that stood like iron against him. When that happened, he could begin to help his people by pointing them to Christ and working to right the wrongs against them.

He was almost to his cabin when he heard a voice behind him. "Marvin?"

He pivoted to see Vetel hurrying after him.

"You want to see me?"

"Ehe." Vetel stopped beside him. For a moment silence hung its curtain between them. "There is something I have to know."

Marvin waited quietly.

"Why didn't you clobber that Aldina and James both? They shamed you in front of everyone."

"It wouldn't have helped anyone."

"And your grandfather?" Awe crept into Vetel's eyes. "He spit in your face!"

"I know."

"I thought you'd kill him for that!"

"I hurt him, Vetel, when I didn't go ahead with the sun dance."

"I wanted to ask about that, too. They were going to make you *okimaaw*. You would have been chief of the reserve by the time the sun dance was finished." He moved closer. "Why, Marvin? What happened to you?"

"It is this Jesus Christ who came into my heart and gave me a new life, Vetel. I tried to tell how it is with me now."

"But we don't understand." There was a strange, searching tone in his voice.

"Come on in the cabin," Marvin said, "and we will talk about these things."

"I think I would like that."

Marvin started forward, a new spring in his step. It was as though the sun had suddenly come up on tomorrow, allowing him to see how he was going to be able to work for his people. It was going to be a wondrous day!